UNSANCTIONED EXPERIMENTS

Ben Credle

This is a collected work of fiction. Any resemblance to any
person, living or dead is purely coincidental.

To my wife Kim, who encourages me to chase my dreams.

CONTENTS

FAMILY SIZE

"Twenty minutes til closing, fellas," Clint calls out, as he empties the trashcan in the men's weight room.

The YMCA is almost empty, just me and Rick on the treadmills, and Mitch over at the free weights, admiring his arms in the mirrors. I reduce the speed on my treadmill down to 2 mph to cool down. Mitch walks into the cardio room and asks loudly, for Rick's benefit, if I checked the weight limit of the treadmill before I got on it. He laughs his stupid laugh, and goes over to Rick for a high-five. Rick casts his eyes at me for an instant, and then half-heartedly fives him. In fact, I *had* checked the weight limit on the treadmill two days ago when I had first started using it, awkwardly wedging my bulk between two machines to read the label at the bottom, but I thought I'd been alone. Had Mitch been watching me? Does he think I *want* to weigh 327 pounds? That's why I'm here sweating at the gym at 4:40 pm on a Saturday.

I go to the locker room to change. I glance up and see Mitch watching me in the mirror as he shaves around his ridiculous fu-manchu mustache with a straight razor. I don't shower here because I don't like people judging my naked body. But I think Mitch wants people to see him naked. He does a little zorro Z in the air with his straight razor as he walks back to his locker.

Two weeks ago, when old Mr. Simmons went missing, the police interviewed all of us gym-goers. The last place anyone had seen him was on the racquetball court across from the weight room. They found his clothes still in his locker. I told the police how Mitch made fun of Mr. Simmons for the Obama sticker on his car, and how he called him a socialist. I told them about Mitch's straight razor. I told them about the huge hunting knife he straps to the outside of his pants like he's on Sons of Anarchy. Does he think I'm going to lie to the police for him? I can't lie to the police.

I hear Mitch loudly tell Rick that he saw me at the KFC across from St. Mary's, and saw me order the family size meal, "and we know he ain't got no wife and kids! Am I right? I think we need to start calling him Family Size!" It's true, I "ain't got no" wife and kids. Does he think I *want* to eat the entire KFC Family Feast myself? Sometimes I can't help myself.

Has Mitch been following me? Watching me order food? Watching me return to my empty apartment? I used to exercise in the morning, but I changed over to afternoons just to get away from Mitch. And now Mitch had switched too. Come to think of it, why was he shaving at night? Why was he even here on a game day? Mitch loved the Bulldogs more than he loved his biceps. I remind myself that this is just paranoia. I'd definitely gotten hyper-vigilant since Mr. Simmons. I look up and see Mitch standing at the end of my alley of lockers. He is watching me with the straight razor still in his hand. I can't leave without going past him. Does he want me to confront him? I can't do confrontation.

I hear the door slam shut; probably Rick leaving. Now I'm alone in the locker room with Mitch. The noise seems to bring him out of a reverie. I refuse to turn toward him, but in my peripheral vision I see him shake his head and turn away. I think I hear him mutter, "Family size." He punches a locker as he leaves and I jump.

I finish getting dressed, gather my things, and close my locker. My breathing is rapid and shallow. Mitch is still at his locker at the end of the next row when the lights suddenly go out. The taser becomes the only light in the room. Mitch hits the floor. I think if I can drag him into the sauna, he'll at least stay warm longer. Mr. Simmons had got cold within 2 hours. I see Mitch look up at me in terror, unable to move his limbs. I feel sorry for him. Does he think I *want* to eat him? Sometimes I can't help myself.

* * * * *

When I saw the call for submissions for Halloween stories in the Athens Flagpole *magazine, I thought there was no way I had time to write a story in a week. But then I thought of the long-suffering protagonist of George Saunders' "The 400 lb CEO," and I decided to take a similar character and go in a decidedly darker direction with him. I wrote the story in a few lunch hours, submitted it, and to my surprise, it won first prize. It's that bit of encouragement that keeps me writing to this day. Thanks,* Flagpole!

TEST SUBJECTS

Looking back, the phone call was the beginning of the end, but I didn't notice the signs at the time. I'd ridden my bike to the top of the only real hill on the island to make the call. The climb wasn't necessary, the phone got decent enough reception down at the lab, but I liked the ride. It got my blood pumping and my mind working better than caffeine or any of its relatives.

While I waited for my breathing to slow enough for conversation, I surveyed the yellowed grass and bushy trees shifting in the ocean wind. This early in summer, the heat was still bearable. The Wardang Bed and Breakfast off to the south had shown no signs of life that early on a weekday, and the morning's stillness made it seem like a scale model of an

English cottage. Even my ranch looked less dusty and run down from up there. The four windmills were in constant motion, but their whooshing wasn't audible from on top of the hill. At night, I might've been able to see the lights from Adelaide off to the east, but in the daylight the mainland had been hazy and indistinct.

I'd expected to get Liam's voicemail, so I was caught a little off guard when he answered. He'd started right in: "Morning, Heyward. I trust you got the package alright?"

"Morning. Yes, picked it up yesterday afternoon. Undamaged, no problems." I'd tried to match his terseness, but it didn't come naturally to me.

"Very good. I need twenty adults injected with thirty mils each. Isolate half of them in a separate pen. How quickly can you have that done?"

I paused. As usual, Liam's rapid delivery made me feel like I wasn't answering quickly enough. "Well, I just let them out for the morning. I'll have to round them back up. Twenty subjects? Say an hour and a half."

"Right, ninety minutes then. Call me when you've got them ready. I'm leaving now, and I should be on the island in four hours."

"Four hours? How do you reckon?"

"We're coming by chopper. Let me know when the subjects are injected," he'd repeated, and hung up.

He did that a lot, just hung up when he was done talking. I remember doing a quick estimate of the fuel cost for a helicopter trip from Melbourne and thinking it was a lot. But I didn't make the next leap of logic: that my little ranch had suddenly become pretty important to Soto Pharma, worth a chopper trip. And Liam had said "We're coming," not "I'm coming." Yeah, in hindsight, that would've been a fine time to run and not look back.

Instead, I climbed back on the bike and pointed it

downhill. The descent back to the farm was fast and hairy; it put whatever misgivings I might've had right out of my mind. I squeezed the brakes and skidded to a stop as soon as I was within the shade of the big gum tree, about a half-kilometer from the compound, then pulled out my phone again. After I punched the icon that my buddy Mathers had made for "Round 'em up" from the screen, I keyed in the option to segregate twenty adults at random. In response, a factory whistle on top of the lab building blew for several seconds, and moments later my herd came ambling in from the fields. As they entered the long alley between the two holding pens, they passed a scanner that read their ear tags. An automated gate opened for the first twenty subjects, sending them to the pen closest to the lab. The remaining eighty or so were sent to the left pen.

They weren't exactly pigs, my subjects. But I haven't come up with anything better to call them yet, and I've tried. From the outside they looked every bit like pigs, but their digestive tracts were as close to Homo Sapiens' as science could make them. The level of genetic modification it takes to achieve this is currently illegal in every country on Earth, but the pigs' value as test subjects for human pharmaceuticals practically guarantees that certain people will be willing to produce them. And that's where I came in.

Wardang Island is a seven by five-kilometer comma off the south Australian coast. It became home to a government bio-lab in the 1990s. But when it turned out to not be isolated enough to keep organisms from reaching the mainland, the government closed the lab. Three decades later, the Aussie government auctioned off the island to raise badly-needed money. The Shaws bought the southern tip, including the nicest beach, and opened their agritourism bed and breakfast. The old lab compound itself was bought by Soto Pharma through an arcane series of intermediaries to hide their ownership. The medical conglomerate started out as a Mexican gray-market pharmacy chain, but had recently made a big push into drug development. Even if the island wasn't quite remote enough for biological quarantine, it was still isolated enough to keep people from snooping around. If you were going to be doing illegal medical testing, you didn't want onlookers.

I had been knocking around that part of the Australian coast for a few months, living on a sailboat, guiding fishing trips, doing a little engineering work — a little bit of anything that paid. When the new owners needed someone local to get the lab up and running, I made myself available. I supervised the installation of the windmills and enough solar panels to make the compound mostly self-sustaining. The new lab equipment came over on my boat. I even ferried the first test subjects. Once the equipment was installed, I figured the job was over, but they asked me to stay on the island for a few weeks until they could find a permanent manager.

Four years later and I was still there. I had the place pretty much to myself, and with help from my pal Mathers in Adelaide, I'd automated my tasks to the point that my actual daily labor was near zero. Occasionally, some scientist-types would stay there for a few days while we tested the next big heartburn drug or spliced up some new embryos. Liam never acknowledged exactly who it was he worked for, from the first time he approached me at the harbor, and I was paid in cash. But the scientists weren't as close-mouthed, and after a few beers they'd mention Soto if you asked the right questions. All in all, it was low-stress work, but I was really nothing but an errand boy. I could never hope for a real career with Soto, because they couldn't officially admit that I existed. I couldn't even go to the company picnic.

The four structures that made up the lab compound were low, green, ranch-style buildings arranged in an L shape. I rode past the machine shop and the bio lab to the bunkhouse, left the bike there, changed into rubber boots, and walked over to the veterinary building to get the new drug. Packed under layers of Styrofoam, I found a glass flask filled with a thin gray liquid that had the dull metallic sheen of silver paint. A handwritten label read, "Demophon." The flask made a horrible scraping noise as I screwed it into the bottom of a pneumatic injection gun. Liam had sent enough for twenty doses of thirty milliliters. I set the gun to 28.5 mils, which would leave me one dose left over, and then headed out into the pen. The pigs were eating lunch, enjoying a sort of vegetable and tofu stew. I'd be lying if I said I'd never eaten it myself — usually on the days that I didn't catch any fish — but it wasn't my favorite.

I made a circuit of the pen, scanning each pig's ear tag with my phone and then injecting it in the shoulder with the silver liquid. I then coaxed ten of them into the adjoining pen. When I was done, there was just under thirty mils of liquid left in the injector.

I drained this into a small bottle and wrote the date on it. This I would put into a box labeled, "Frozen Eggrolls" in the back of the little freezer in my bedroom, beside a secret sample of every other drug Liam had sent me. Mathers had put this idea in my head. It was my little insurance policy for the potential day the company decided this clandestine lab and its too-knowledgeable caretaker represented an unacceptable liability.

With that little bit of skullduggery out of the way, I called Liam to let him know I was done, then tidied the place up and began the hunt for a clean shirt.

The pigs heard the chopper before I did and started squealing. The pilot had the good sense to set down out of sight behind a slight rise. Liam eventually came striding over the hill. Tall, thin, and with the hair of a local news anchor, he wasn't one for idle conversation, so I led him directly to the subject pen. Liam pulled rubber boots on over his dress shoes and climbed in. He donned a tiny headset-mounted video camera and then produced a silver box the size of a brick from inside his jacket. Holding it out in front of him as if he were afraid of it, he walked slowly around the pen, pausing next to each pig for several seconds, even following the pig if it moved away.

Within a minute, two of the first subjects he'd approached began bleating loudly. By the time Liam had approached all ten of them, the first two had begun jerking violently. Then several others started convulsing.

The first pig fell over; its head twitched for a moment, then it lay still. By this time all the pigs were behaving hysterically, and Liam jumped back outside the fence and began pacing the pen's perimeter, holding the silver box out toward the animals.

"What the hell, Liam?" I blurted, "I'd say your new drug doesn't work."

Liam looked up and gave me a smirk. "We're trying something a little different. Not looking to cure heartburn this time." He looked at his watch and put the box back in his jacket pocket. Six pigs lay motionless on the ground; the other four lay convulsing. "Let's get a drink and I'll tell you all about it." He began walking toward the bunkhouse. I stood staring at the dead and dying animals, unable to absorb it. "C'mon," Liam called, and slowed to wait for me.

"So you're testing poisonous medicine?" I asked. "Doesn't seem like there's a helluva market for that."

Liam paused to answer me: "The boys in the white coats have built a remotely-activated drug delivery system. What you just saw was our own proprietary variant of a flesh-eating virus. And you're right, there's no real market for that by itself, but what we've done is encapsulate the virus in tiny carbon nanotube cages. The cages prevent the virus from interacting with outside cells. Again, not something anyone would want to buy. The marketable part is that the cages are built to resonate and shake apart if they're given just the right frequency input. You ever hear of the Tacoma Narrows Bridge in the States?"

I nodded. Every engineering student had watched the video of the bridge that had swayed and bucked and eventually collapsed, thought to be due to a moderate wind at exactly the wrong frequency.

Liam pulled the silver box back out of his pocket and held it toward me. "This is just a radio transmitter. All it takes is about twenty seconds of the correct frequency and the little carbon cages shake themselves apart, then our virus is loose inside the body. Of course, the stuff is ungodly expensive to produce, but our military branch has taken an interest, so we've got a considerable budget."

That explained the helicopter.

Liam was getting excited, warming to his subject: "Imagine your enemy is squirreled away in caves or something, and you can't get to them. But you can get some of this stuff in their food or water supply. A conventional poison would kill the first person who ate it, and nobody else would touch it. But our stuff has an on/off switch, you see. You can wait for the whole group to tuck in to a meal, or even several meals, and then you send your radio waves at them. The effective range is tens of kilometers, depending on how big a transmitter you want to employ."

Liam was talking faster and higher. He was nearly gleeful as we approached the bunkhouse. "Or think of it in an occupation situation. You dose the town's water supply, and now your soldiers can walk the streets with just a radio on their hip. If anything goes sour, they can kill everyone within a hundred meter radius, but with no explosions or property damage, and no risk of hurting a friendly. We're calling it Demophon. Named for one of the Greeks that hid inside the Trojan horse. Get it?" He looked at me expectantly.

I just nodded, unsure what to say.

Undeterred, he went on: "Of course, we've loads more to do – establish the lethal dose, see how long it stays effective in the body. Our models show it should be a quick killer for three to five days after ingestion. But even out to a few weeks, it could cause a slow death, or at least severe illness. So we're going to keep you very busy for quite a while, testing it."

By this time we'd reached the porch. Liam bent to take off his boots. I walked inside and saw two sturdy-looking men standing in my living room. They wore military fatigues with no insignia at all. Probably contractors. Large guys, all muscles and crew cuts. They didn't acknowledge me, just looked right over my shoulder at Liam, who had come in behind me.

"Like I said, this is a military project now," Liam said quietly. "Our friends are here to assess the lab's security. This is a recon trip, but they'll be back in a few days to stay until the testing wraps up."

"You guys need a beer?" I offered, trying to sound unintimidated.

The contractors continued to look at Liam, who answered for everyone: "Too right. The flight out was a little rough."

I crossed to the kitchen and came back carrying two cans of Victoria Bitter. As I reached out to give the first ogre his beer, his hand came up and clamped around my arm just above the elbow. Lightning fast, his other hand pressed an injection gun to my shoulder and pulled the trigger. Then he released his grip and took a step back, watching me as if I were likely to bite him. The whole engagement was so unexpected that I had no idea how to react. I spun around to see the other ogre with a pistol in his hand, pointed at the floor. He scanned me up and down, looking for any excuse to raise the gun. My guess was he'd put a lot of bullets into people who thought they were quicker than him.

"What the hell was that?"

Liam held up his hands in a calming gesture. "I do apologize for that, Heyward," he said unapologetically, " but this is a sensitive project. Our military partners needed assurance that you wouldn't experience any sudden wanderlust during the next few weeks of tests. Strictly a precaution. In a month, we should know all we need to know about Demophon. Then these chaps will clear out and we'll have a laugh about this. Until then, just remember that you've got the same thing in you that the subjects in the pen have, and if we think you're doing anything to compromise our secrecy, well, you understand…"

With that, they all walked out. The ogres flanked Liam and scanned for threats. Liam, completely unconcerned, picked lint off his sweater as he walked. I stood watching them go, trying to crush the unopened beers in my hands, until I heard the chopper whump-whump-whump away.

* * *

I walked outside in a daze, and wandered to the pen to look at the ten surviving pigs: the control subjects. They looked fine… for now. But what if something in their bodies could break down the carbon cages? What if the cages in my body were dissolving right now? I took a deep breath to stave off total panic. It seemed pretty clear that even if I survived, my services would cease to be needed, and soon. My value as experienced labor would look vanishingly small stacked next to the risk of me letting the wrong people know what was happening on the island. I was also sure the beefing-up of security was meant to make me a permanent resident of the island for the rest of my possibly short life.

The pigs looked up at me expectantly, as if nothing had

happened. Completely unaware of their impending doom, they just wanted a snack. They were born on the island, and they would die on it, never knowing anything different. They looked happy, and I envied them.

But I *did* know about the larger world. I might die soon, but I didn't have to do it there, as an errand boy to a preening corporate sociopath. I decided, with unexpected clarity and resolve, that my only real option was to leave while I still could.

I packed myself a bag, assuming I would never be coming back. It surprised me how few things I owned that I would be sorry to lose. There were a lot of books I loved, but they were easily replaceable. The thought of being eaten alive from the inside overshadowed a lot of sentimental attachment.

I was a long way from the dock when I saw my boat wasn't there. When did they have time to take it? When I reached the dock, I saw a piece of paper held down with a rock. It read, "Your boat will be returned at the end of the testing." No signature. And probably no real chance of my boat being returned either.

My face felt hot and my heart pounded. Real panic began to set in. It had felt abstract before, but now there was no denying I was a prisoner.

There was one other way off the island. My neighbors at the bed and breakfast made a trip to the mainland most mornings to pick up and drop off guests. I hated to involve the Shaws in my dilemma, but I didn't see any other choice. I called and explained that my boat was having trouble, and they were happy to give me a lift the next morning.

The boat trip was uneventful and anticlimactic. I watched the island recede, but it didn't really tug at my heartstrings. Looking at it just reminded me of my unexpected injection. I realized that the island hadn't been home at all, just a stopover — a four-year layover.

Of course, every time I burped I thought it was the virus attacking me, so to distract myself I chatted with Jane as she drove. I realized I couldn't just disappear without giving her some sort of heads-up.

"Listen," I started, "the company I work for has been talking about bringing in a new team to run the lab, and they're pretty paranoid about security. So if you see strangers up there, you're probably better off leaving them alone." The last thing I wanted was the Shaws getting dragged into this.

I spent the rest of the trip thinking about my next move. I was still convinced that leaving the island made sense, but it would be a pointless gesture if they just killed me tomorrow somewhere else. If I was going to stay alive, I was going to have to be smart.

I had some ideas.

After we tied up the boat, I took a cab out to Mathers' place. As far as I could tell, Mathers was at work when I got there, sat in the center of his shop, surrounded by several computers, talking on a headset. When he saw me he waved and mouthed, "Five minutes," while pointing to his watch in big dramatic gestures. He had three TVs mounted to the wall behind me, all showing different news stations. The empty bottles on his desk indicated he was on at least his third iced latte of the day; his plump body radiated nervous energy.

It wouldn't be quite right to call Mathers a computer hacker. The fact was, he approached his whole life looking for the better, easier, cleverer way to do everything. Computers were just included in his general attitude. And if large organizations didn't want him to do a particular thing, he needed – in a way that was part of his DNA – to find a way to do it. He spent some of his time getting paid to test corporate security, and he was exactly who I needed.

When I told him my story, he became even more agitated than usual.

"Jesus, man!" Mathers barked. "As soon as they find out you're gone, they'll start transmitting your radio death sentence. You need to put some serious distance between you and them."

"That was my initial thought, too. But then I figured there's no future in running from the company and waiting for them to catch me. When is it safe? I've spent four years doing whatever they tell me. If I run now, I'll spend the rest of my life letting them control what I do. I need to put a stop to this crap. It's time for me to be in control of myself."

I added hopefully: "That's why I need your help…"

Mathers sat back, took a second to reassess me, then slurped at his cold coffee: "Right… I can get behind that."

As long as he'd known me, I had sought the path of least resistance, but now I was showing him a different side. As the new parameters for his mental model of me began to sink in, he nodded his head more and more vigorously, until he started rocking in his chair. "Yeah, okay. What'd you have in mind?" he asked.

I told him. I had a vague and fuzzy goal, and Mathers provided the very clear and concrete ideas of how to achieve it. We spent the entire day planning, Mathers teaching his new disciple as many relevant tricks as he could from the gospel according to Johnny Long. After a trip to the Mega-Mart for supplies, I loaded up Mathers' ute and set out driving a little before midnight. Mathers wished me luck and came outside to watch me go. I scanned his face to see if he really believed I had a chance or not. I couldn't tell.

The drive from Adelaide to Melbourne is seven hours of monotony, and in the dark I didn't even get a view of the ocean. With no sleep and a handful of those quasi-legal stimulants that truckers take, it was even worse. But there was no time for sleep. The only way this scheme had any prayer of working was if we did it now. If Soto Pharma got an inkling that something was amiss, all bets weren't quite off, but my odds got ridiculously long.

The Aussie landscape revealed by my headlights still felt slightly wrong to my North American mind. The distances were too big. The spindly gum trees were too far apart and had a definite Seussian shape to them.

As I drove east, Mathers was heading west, taking my phone back to Wardang. He had forwarded all my calls to the new phone in my pocket, but if the Soto security boys took the trouble to track my phone's location, it would still show up right where it was supposed to be.

Soto Pharma headquarters is west of town in a dusty industrial area called Laverton North. I parked Mathers' ute at a gas station five kilometers away. I was a little early, so I went inside and bought a hideous energy drink the color of antifreeze and a pack of cigarettes.

From satellite photos, we had learned everything we could about the company campus. The pictures showed cars lined up at the gated entrance as guards checked IDs. Since my goal involved getting inside the building, this had been a cause for concern for me, but Mathers was unfazed: "Look, their security plan, like at most companies, depends on you walking up to a guard and saying, 'I don't belong here, will you let me in?' It basically keeps out door-to-door salesmen. But they're never going to see you coming."

It had made so much sense when he said it.

A few minutes later, I walked around the corner and caught the 8:20 bus. It was half filled with sleepy people on their way to work. After two stops, about twelve of us got off in front of the Soto gates. We were all dressed basically alike: khakis and polo shirts, the uniform of the anonymous office employee. The other thing we had in common was a colorful laminated Soto Pharma badge clipped to our shirts. It had taken Mathers about two minutes of searching online to find photos from a company office party that showed Soto ID badges in enough detail for us to make a reasonable fake.

The guard glanced up as we approached, and hit his buzzer to unlock the pedestrian gate. We entered in a line. I'd inserted myself about mid-pack, my heart beating against my chest like it wanted out. The guy in front of me held the gate open for me. I managed to find something to look at other than the security guard. I held the gate for the girl behind me and I was in, just like that.

Hurdle number one was cleared.

Past the gate, my adopted herd ambled through the parking lot toward the wide three-story main building. I peered over the people in front of me to see inside. As the front door was pulled open, I could see turnstiles within, each with a line of people waiting to slide their badge through a scanner. This was a big problem, because my fake badge didn't have the barcode, or magnetic strip, or whatever it was the scanners were reading.

But Mathers had anticipated this, and now it was time to see how good our Plan B was.

I stopped walking and pulled out my newly-purchased pack of cigarettes. I used the time it took to open them to keep watching the herd in front of me. Just as I had hoped, one of my bus-mates veered off toward the right of the building as he lit a smoke of his own.

I followed at a discreet distance, and saw two other people standing near a side door, all puffing away. As I neared the group, I pulled out my phone and pretended to listen to a message. I stood a little apart from the group, turned away from them, and exhaled through my lit cigarette to burn it down. I didn't want to risk inhaling and end up in a suspicious coughing fit.

After a long two minutes, the smokers began to head for the door, which was propped open with a rock. I stubbed out my cigarette, keeping the phone to my ear, and allowed someone to hold the door open for me. I gave him a half-smile and a little "thank you" nod, and I was inside the building. Hurdle number two... cleared.

I hung back as the other smokers walked ahead of me. The realization that people in this building had a plan in place to kill me was more than a little alarming. In fact, it weighed on me like bags of concrete. I was having trouble breathing, and had to fight the urge to turn around and run.

When the door slammed closed behind me, I almost yelled. Instead, I took the deepest breath I could and forced myself to walk forward. It was cold inside, and quiet. Mathers had given me some basic advice on how to navigate the building, but all I could remember was "Improvise and don't look lost."

The smell of cigarette smoke was gradually replaced by that of cleaning chemicals. The long hall was awash in greenish fluorescent light, and seemed to lead toward the front atrium, the place I had just gone to some trouble to avoid. So I turned right at the first side passage, feeling lost and conspicuous. I passed a few people in the hall but no one paid me any real attention. Finally, hanging in a little black frame on the wall, I found what I needed: the emergency evacuation map, which showed me the layout of the building and even labeled the departments.

I muttered an occasional, "Right... sure," into my phone as I looked at the map with feigned disinterest, learning there was nothing I wanted on this floor. Customer service and shipping were of no use to me, but I did locate the stairs, at the end of the next east-west hall. They were far from the elevators, so I had the stairwell to myself.

At the second floor, I poked my head out the door, and seeing the coast relatively clear, emerged and walked the long empty hall until I found another map. This time I was in luck.

Engineering and R&D were up here, and they shared a common breakroom with the conference room at the front of the building.

Keeping my head down, I walked past the breakroom into the bathroom, then straight into a stall to prepare for my big play. Out of my messenger bag I pulled the glass vial that held my backup dose of Demophon. I used my phone to take a picture of the full container, and then put the vial carefully into my pants pocket. Next, I pulled a coffee cup out, slung the bag over my shoulder, and headed out the door toward the breakroom.

There were two people already there when I walked in, but I didn't recognize either of them. I didn't really know what I would have done if one of them had been Liam.

I crossed to the coffee maker and poured myself a half cup, then I stood next to the sugar with my back to the two women. Carefully, I pulled the flask out of my pocket and poured most of the drug into my cup, hoping I wasn't attracting attention.

Finally, the two ladies finished their discussion of the weather and left, so I picked up the coffee pot, placed it next to my empty flask on the counter, and took a picture of it, making sure to get the Soto company bulletin board in the background to prove where I was. I had the pictures I wanted: one of a flask full of Demophon, and one of the empty flask next to a full coffee pot. Seeing those, Liam could only come to one conclusion.

I could leave, my mission accomplished, just like Mathers and I had planned it. But to leave now wouldn't quite be enough. I didn't want to walk out worrying that Liam might call my bluff.

And the way to prevent that was to not be bluffing.

Hearing footsteps approaching, I put the coffee pot back and continued pretending to put sugar in my cup. A tall frizzy-haired nerd-type came in and grabbed a water bottle from the refrigerator.

As he was leaving, he glanced back at me, and then paused. "Heyward?"

Every muscle in my back stiffened, but I turned around casually. He was smiling at me. His name was Siggy; he'd stayed on the island for a few days once during a drug trial. We'd had a pretty good time boozing it up at night.

"I thought it was you!" he said. "What are you doing here?"

His tone wasn't accusing, but the question hung out there. So I improvised.

"Siggy, hey! I've got a big meeting with Liam on a new trial," I answered. Then, lowering my voice: "Kinda hush-hush. If you see him, tell him we're ready in the conference room whenever he is." Siggy seemed to completely miss the fact that under no circumstances would the company ever want me to come here. I pushed on, not giving him time to make that connection. "Maybe we can catch a drink after work tonight. I'll come find you after the meeting."

"Sounds good. I'll tell Randy, too. There's a great bar not far down Geelong."

"Perfect. I'll come find you after this," I repeated, and then headed out the door I had come in, ending the conversation.

Outside in the hall, I waited for ten agonizing seconds, looking down at my coffee cup, and then went right back into the breakroom.

Siggy had left by the door that led to engineering, and my time was very quickly running out. He might already be telling Liam I was here.

Without hesitating, I emptied my dosed coffee back into the coffee pot, threw the cup in the trash, and hurried out the door. I quick-walked around the corner, then into the stairwell, taking the stairs two at a time. Before I got to the bottom, my phone was vibrating. I didn't answer. I hustled out the side door to the smoking area and leaned back against the wall.

My phone showed one missed call, from Liam's number.

I emailed my two newly-taken pictures to him, then began walking toward the front gate, calling Liam back as I went. He picked up on the first ring.

"Where are you?" he snapped.

"I'm in Melbourne, but that's not your most important concern right now. I just sent you an email, showing me returning some company property to you. It seems I had some left over from your military test. By now you've got some new control subjects for your experiment, so I don't think you're going to want to broadcast on the frequency that breaks open the cages. Might look bad at your next employee review – you know, killing your co-workers and so forth." I waited, but he didn't reply. "You still there?"

A long silence, then, "Yes."

"Good. Listen, I'm going to need you to keep paying me for the next year or so. That will make sure I don't have to do anything desperate to pay my bills... like selling what's left in this flask to your competitors. I'll be in touch if I think of anything else I need. You guys have fun playing army, okay? Oh, and tell Siggy we'll have to have that drink another night."

I hung up. I wasn't really interested in listening to him threaten me or yell or whatever he had in mind.

By this time, I had made it back to the guard shack. I waved and the guard buzzed the gate open. Out on the street, I took off my fake Soto badge and started walking to where I'd left Mathers' ute. I had some thinking to do. Liam couldn't activate the virus in my body without risking unknown lives in his own office. And he probably wouldn't send the military guys looking for me, because he wouldn't want to admit what had just happened. He'd tell them that I'd been transferred or something.

Either way, it would be smartest for me to never go back to Wardang Island.

The November sun warmed my skin, and a breeze made me think of open water. Yesterday I could never leave the island, and now today I could never go back. But I had the whole rest of the world to choose from, and that seemed like a pretty good trade.

* * * * *

This is one of my earliest stories. I first read about Wardang Island in an article in The New Scientist *around 1995. The Australian government had tried using the island to test an anti-rabbit virus, but the virus reached the mainland before they were ready. Then in 2002, I worked in Melbourne for a month installing some cracker-packaging machines. Compared to the US, everything there was similar but intriguingly different. It was so compelling that I had to set a story there somehow.*

This story received an Honorable Mention from the Writers of the Future Contest in 2019.

THE TOURIST

When people asked Peter what it was like to work up there, he usually talked about the peace, and the silent views of the majestic earth, or the tension of trying to catch something moving and spinning. Or the inescapable smell of ozone and the monotony. But sometimes, after a drink or three, he would talk about what it was like to be trapped in an orbiting cylinder with a homicidal megalomaniac, which is what people really wanted to hear in the first place.

The day they wanted to hear about started out full of promise. The shuttle came up that morning like it did every two weeks, picking up and dropping off. Peter spent a lot of the morning thinking about Raquel. In fact, ever since he saw her name on the shuttle schedule, he hadn't thought about much else. Peter looked up to see his boss, Roger, floating toward him. Roger had said something and Peter had missed it. "What?" he asked.

Roger grabbed a strap near Peter to stop his motion and said, "I was just telling everyone to stow their personal items before the shuttle docks. It's not every day we get a tourist, and this could be a real win for us." Roger pushed past Peter and the other two Capture Technicians to the crew-end of the module, where he began stowing anything that wasn't company issued, no matter whose it was. Over his shoulder, he kept talking, "I don't have to tell you how much it would mean if we could get him to upgrade to an Extended Stay, or a You Catch It package. Module 4 had three Extended Stays last quarter. If we could start pulling numbers like that, nobody would have to be worried about layoffs over here. So we need to do anything we can to make him feel welcome."

Peter sighed involuntarily and went back to ignoring Roger. The three Techs sat back to back to back, watching their monitors, which were laid out like a ring inside the midpoint of the cylindrical module. On either side of him, Leroy and Humpty resumed their conversation about the intricacies of the above-ground pools from Walmart.

"I'm telling you, I had that thing 3 years, and it ain't leaked a drop of water," Leroy said. "'Course, the water's as black as Peter's asshole 'cause the pump quit working!" He laughed so loud it startled Peter.

Humpty snorted. "Well, I guess I better figure out how to fix them pumps, 'cause I know she's gonna buy one before I get back down. Every time I'm up here, she buys some kinda shit I gotta work on."

And so it went, for two more hours, until the shuttle showed up.

* * *

From the outside, OrbitSweeper Module 3 looked like a

Pringles can had sprouted tentacles: a fat, gray cylinder with six long multi-jointed arms coming out of its middle. The shuttle navigated around the spidery arms and docked at the command end. Roger repeatedly wet his lips and smoothed his thinning red hair as he waited at the airlock to usher the tourist aboard and start the technical tour. The man who came through the pressure door was tall, with short graying hair. He had the slack heft of an aging ex-football player. But mostly, he looked like a fairly normal guy, which was good. A lot of times, the kind of guys who could afford to spend the cost of a large house on a joyride to space turned out to be serious weirdos. His name was Walter Camden, and as Roger had repeatedly reminded them, he'd made a bunch of money in vending machines. Or washing machines. Roger repeatedly reminded them about a lot of things; it was impossible to pay attention to all of them. Peter felt like, perversely, the more often Roger told him something, the less likely he was to remember it.

"Welcome aboard, Mr. Camden," Roger said, shaking the tourist's hand. "How was your trip up?"

"Not bad at all, Roger," answered Camden, smiling easily. "Where can I throw my stuff?"

"Oh, we'll get that for you. What about a drink?"

Camden nodded, and the two of them pushed off toward the kitchen. Roger glided there in the single fluid movement of a guy who'd spent months in orbit, while Camden struggled to keep up using the short jerky pushes of a first-timer. After Camden cleared out of the way, Raquel floated through the hatch, her glossy dark hair tied up in some complicated shape, wearing Peter's favorite shirt. It read "Molon Labe" across the front, on stretchy lycra tight enough to accent her boobs. If you were a boob guy, then zero-gravity was a beautiful place to be. Peter wasn't necessarily a boob guy, but he was a Raquel guy. He'd googled "Molon Labe", and it meant she was a gun nut, which only increased his fascination.

She was still beautiful. Peter had decided she was beautiful when he'd first seen her five months ago. But when he wasn't around her, he wondered if she was really that attractive, or if she just benefitted from the artificial markup a girl got in a mostly male environment. No, Raquel was actually beautiful. The big dark wide-set eyes and full lips were perfectly in proportion with her small athletic figure. It made Peter even more curious, because attractive women who could make it through astronaut training could go to the glamour jobs at Virgin Galactic or at least the prestige jobs at the International Space Station. But here she was, catching debris at OrbitSweeper, home of the space garbagemen.

Pouches of water in hand, Roger began showing the tourist around the upstream end of the module, starting with the tiny kitchen and then the four crew compartments. Each was basically the size of a coffin, which was a little unnerving since they doubled as the escape pods. The guest compartment, over at the command end of the module, was twice as big, about the size of an airplane bathroom. Meanwhile, Humpty disengaged from the gray control sleeves to go pack his stuff for the trip back down. Raquel floated over and took Humpty's place at the arm controls. She still moved with the grace and efficiency of some exotic sea creature, even after her two weeks on the ground. Peter had a few minutes before Roger's tour reached them at Capture Control. He caught Raquel's eye, and got as far as, "Hey Raquel! How's it-" before Leroy talked over him.

"Baby, I had a dream about you," Leroy began in his booming Texas drawl. Peter and Humpty turned to hear where this was going. "You were riding a elephant naked. I never wanted to be a elephant so bad."

Raquel turned away from him with her tight dangerous

smile, the one that hinted that you might get cut, but didn't answer, just typed at the controls. She was a little scary like that. Peter saw a small window flashing at the bottom corner of his monitor. It was an instant message from Raquel:

MIGHT HAVE 2 KILL LEROY. WILL U HELP?

Peter struggled for a clever response, delighted that he and Raquel had this secret exchange going. With five people jammed in a module the size of a school bus, any kind of private communication was hard to come by. With his right hand Peter typed onto the tiny keypad on the left wrist of the control sleeves:

U MIGHT HAVE TO GET IN LINE.

* * *

There were two extremes of techs up here. There were the guys who were savant-like with the robot arms, who could catch anything that came by, no matter how oddly shaped or crazily spinning. Those guys tended to not have the greatest social skills. Then there were the pretty people, who maybe weren't extraordinary at the catch, but who looked the part of Joe Astronaut, and represented OrbitSweeper well. Peter was somewhere in the middle, but skewed toward the pretty people.

Roger did his best to keep his pretty people on duty when tourists showed up, and keep his savants hidden away. This is why Roger scheduled Humpty, or as he called him, Adam, to leave with the shuttle that brought the tourist up. Once on a bet, Humpty had put a Rubik's cube out the airlock, and solved it with the mechanical capture arms. It took him about 6 minutes. But in conversation with strangers, Humpty came across as a robotic hick, with his skinny limbs and military buzz cut. Roger probably would've preferred to ship Leroy down, too. Leroy skewed to the savant end of the spectrum. He was not unattractive despite carrying quite a few extra pounds, and he was certainly charismatic, but you couldn't trust him to keep the conversation appropriate in front of the visitors. And his approach to females, any female, was so outlandish it was almost comical. Unfortunately, it apparently worked often enough that he never gave it a rest. But Roger couldn't lose all his best catchers, not during a high-profile assignment like they had now. Peter had heard Roger asking Leroy to keep it clean around the tourist, but it was probably wishful thinking.

Roger brought the tourist toward the Capture Stations, and pointed to Peter, Leroy and Raquel as if they were zoo animals. "And this is the reason we're all up here. Our Capture Technicians watch the monitors for any incoming orbital debris. If it fits the criteria of what we can safely capture, they'll use either the robot arms or the netting to grab it. Then they'll stow it against the hull, where it becomes a little bit more armor for us." Roger paused to let the "armor" comment sink in, hoping it had the intended effect of making it seem like they were in constant and exciting danger up here. "If you want to watch, it looks like Peter has an incoming now. Peter, can you talk us through the capture, for our guest's benefit?"

Peter cleared his throat. "Sure. If you'll look here, the radar has picked up a small incoming at my 10 o'clock. Our sensors can estimate size and speed, and guess at mass. The green outline means the computer thinks it's small and slow enough that it's a good candidate for a catch." He pointed with his chin toward his center screen, and the tourist studied it like there might be a test later.

"What's that flashing number, off to the side?" Camden pointed.

"That's the estimated spin. Some items are spinning fast enough that it could damage us to try and catch them. The bad news is that the sensors aren't great at reading the spin, so the flashing means the computer thinks it might be spinning too fast, but it isn't sure. Since this one's small enough, it's worth a try." Peter was quiet then, all concentration, as he shrugged his shoulders to loosen up his arms within the articulated plastic control sleeves, then nodded his head sharply to snap the VR headset down over his face, like a welding helmet. His center monitor screen had switched to a first-person view. The onlookers could see the robot arms, shown in the left and right edges of the display, doing their impression of Peter's shoulder shrug.

The chunk of debris came into view, and it was highlighted a dark amber now. Peter spoke a little louder, "Orange. Repeat, orange. Need backup."

Raquel and Leroy both turned back to their own screens and snapped their visors down. Each of them swung one arm downward in the bulky control sleeves and mimed grabbing something and lifting it up, causing their capture arms to pick up their nets.

Roger directed the tourist's attention to their screens. "The orange color indicates the piece is definitely spinning fast. So now, both of the other Operators will position nets behind Peter's arms, in case the object gets past him, or breaks up, or worst case, tears the capture arm off. Ordinarily we might just let a piece like this go past us." Roger glanced at the tourist while he paused for emphasis. "But this week, we've been contracted to sit upstream of the Hubble telescope, to provide protection while they open it up to upgrade it."

"Really?" asked Camden. "I hadn't realized that thing was still up here."

"Oh, yes; it never really stopped working," said Roger. "It just got overshadowed by the newer telescopes. But with this optics upgrade, it's supposed to be back on the leading edge."

"That's really interesting. How close are we to it? Can we see it?"

"Well, we're about a hundred and fifty meters upstream of it, so we can block anything that's headed toward it. We don't have a lot of windows on the module, but you can probably catch a glimpse of it through the dock area once the shuttle's gone."

"I'd like that," Camden said.

Peter's head moved as he tracked the object in his headset. He raised both arms like he was trying to catch an overthrown football, and the two robotic arms on the outside of the module mimicked his motions. The left arm suddenly flashed toward the orange projectile, unexpectedly stretching in the process, and the jaws clamped onto it. The right arm quickly came up to steady the object. The spectators let out a collective breath.

"Nice!" Camden said. "You expect to hear some kind of sound when he catches it. Too many movies, I guess."

Peter welded the curved chunk of aluminum to some previously captured junk at the crew-end of the module and announced: "Seven centimeters."

"Sorry to hear that, Peter," Leroy said. "But you know it ain't all about length…"

"Something that size could've really torn up the telescope," Roger broke in, before Leroy could develop that thought any further. "Probably a piece of a spent booster stage. Great work, Peter." With that, Roger ushered Camden toward the command-end of the module to finish the tour.

The three techs went back to work, watching their monitors and catching the occasional object almost unconsciously. With a tourist around, the techs kept their chit-chat to a minimum, and Peter got into a sort of trance, literally staring into space. The robotic arms on the sides of the module felt like natural extensions of himself. It was times like these, in this no-mind state, when he could catch with the best of them. But every few minutes, Raquel's faint vanilla scent would overcome the ever-present heated-metal smell of space, and Peter would lose his trance. He tensed up, achingly self-conscious of every move. Peter finally gathered his wits and cleared his throat, preparing to ask Raquel what she'd done during her downtime. Again, Leroy cut in before Peter even got a word out. "Hey girl, what was that Camden dude like on the ride up?"

"Nervous," she said with her German accent, "like all of them. Staring at my tits, and acting like he wasn't."

"If you and me were in that shuttle for six hours, I'd need IV fluids when we got up here," Leroy interjected. Then, to Peter, "I wanna know when he's gonna loosen up. Usually the first thing they do is start turning backflips and shit. If it was me, I'd be trying to figure out a way to join the three-hundred-mile-high club with Raquel. But this guy acts like he's up here for a prostate exam."

Raquel let that go without reaction, and said, "But he was quiet-nervous, not talky-nervous like some of them." Her accent made it hard to catch every word. On her it sounded exotic. "He did get a little chatty when I told him we were parked by the Hubble. He asked..." she trailed off as Roger and Camden floated towards them. Roger passed easily through the ring of catchers, but Camden bumped into Peter, then grabbed the chair to stop his motion. Once he'd steadied himself, he watched the monitors over Peter's shoulder.

"How big are the pieces you typically catch?" he asked. "It's hard to get any sense of scale just seeing them on the monitors."

"Well, a lot of the random things that we spot with our sensors range up to about eight centimeters across," Peter began. "If they're bigger than ten, the ground stations can track them, and they'll warn us ahead of time. Sometimes Ground even knows where specific pieces came from; they pay extra for certain ones. Military stuff. But that's pretty rare." Roger, seeing Camden was in good hands, headed off toward the kitchen.

"And how often do you catch something?" Camden asked.

Peter tilted his head while he thought about it. "It averages out to about one object every twenty minutes, but that's misleading. We might go hours with nothing, and then get a whole barrage of junk at once." Then, as Roger had taught him, Peter attempted to steer the conversation back to the tourist himself. Everyone liked to talk about themselves. "How long have you wanted to go into space?"

"Oh…" Camden paused, and seemed a little flustered that he didn't have a quick answer. "I guess as a kid I played astronaut like everybody did, especially growing up outside Houston. But then I had to get a regular job, and I forgot all about it. But once my company made a pretty good chunk of money, space started to seem like something I could actually do." He stopped, lost in thought. Then he turned back. "What about you? Always wanted to come up here?"

"Me? No, nothing that… romantic," Peter answered. "I came up for the money. I had the grades and passed the physical, and it seemed like a cool thing I could do until I figured out what I wanted to be when I grew up. But once you've been up here a while, it grows on you. The quiet, the limitless expanse, the…" Peter looked over at Camden, who was looking away toward Raquel, interested either in her or her screen.

Camden snapped out of it. "I'm sorry, what were you saying?"

Peter decided he might as well push for the sale before he lost the tourist's attention completely. "I was saying you really need to be up here for more than a few hours to appreciate it. When you're up here a while, the quiet sort of soaks into you. That and the weightlessness make it very zen. That's when you really start to look into space, and feel it looking back." Peter hesitated, not wanting to push too soon, then decided the awkward silence was worse. "Have you thought about staying up longer? If you decide to, I can even let you strap in at a Capture Station. You get to keep anything you catch, as a..." Peter almost said "souvenir," but remembered Roger telling them that "souvenir" reminded the focus groups of tacky gift shops full of shot glasses and airbrushed license plates. "...as a keepsake to remember the experience," he finished hopefully.

Camden thought for an excruciating count of three, which gave Peter plenty of time to prepare for the inevitable rejection. "That sounds pretty good. I could probably clear my schedule for another day. What do we need to do to make that happen?"

Peter was caught off guard, and tried not to let his excitement show. "Well, we just need to let Roger know. The shuttle will go ahead and drop supplies at the other module without you, and then pick you up in eighteen hours. Or twenty-four, or whatever. It just breaks into six hour increments to hit the right landing window."

His first Extended Stay sale! "I think there are some forms you have to sign, too. You're really going to be glad you did this. Roger!" he shouted, maybe a little louder than necessary in the small space.

Roger pushed-off toward them, carrying juice boxes, looking ready to apologize for whatever offensive thing Leroy might've said. "What is it, Peter?"

Peter answered, "Roger, Mr. Camden has said he'd like to do an Extended Stay." Turning to Camden, he went on, "Do you think you'd like to try your hand at a Capture Station while you're here?" It was important that Camden confirm this in front of the group, so there was no question who would get the sales commission.

Camden smiled and nodded slowly, then said, "Yeah, I

think I'd like that. But only if you and Raquel here will ride shotgun with me." Roger's eyebrows rose to their full upward limit, followed by a smile and some more obsequious back-patting.

As Roger ushered Camden toward his quarters, Leroy said, "Goddam, Pete, your ass-kissing finally paid off!"

Raquel nodded, "Nice work, Peter." From her it sounded like, "Pete-air."

Peter tried to downplay it, but his grin was ear-to-ear. "Thanks. Maybe now Roger really will shut up about cutbacks." If he caught anything for the rest of his shift, he didn't remember it.

* * *

Dinner on the module was usually a solitary event. Since everyone worked and slept on staggered shifts, it wasn't easy to have a big group meal. But on shuttle days, everyone made an effort to eat together. And now, with an Honored Guest, they pulled out all the stops. Peter dialed down the too-bright LEDs to give a little atmosphere. Roger even dug into his private stash of wine, which was as fancy as it got up here, even if it did come in individual foil pouches like a Capri Sun.

Camden and Roger had lamb, also from Roger's stash, and the scent temporarily overrode the background smell of plastic and sweat. Leroy, Peter, and Raquel made do with their regular-crew choices, which were basically military rations, since they were optimized for small size and light weight. The five diners clustered around the small fold-out table, trying not to elbow each other.

Roger broke the silence. "This is nice. And after dinner, we might get a view of the northern lights, weather permitting. They're really breathtaking from up here."

Leroy let out a choking laugh, and they all looked at him. He was still chuckling when he said, "Breathtaking? Ain't that what they said set off that psycho on Module 4 last year? Got all swept away with the lights and then he tried to strangle-"

"We're not really sure what happened," Roger broke in. "We may never know. But let's not worry about that right now. Walter, have you ever seen the Aurora Borealis? Is it ok if I call you Walter?"

"As a matter of fact, I did see it one time from a boat. But I'll make sure to catch that," Camden replied, and then switched gears. "So what do you guys do for fun on the ground? Raquel, I noticed your shirt. You a shooter?"

Raquel looked down at her shirt, said, "Yeah, you could say that," then smiled and pulled her right sleeve up to the elbow, showing off a tattoo of an embellished Colt 1911 pistol. It was so new that the skin was still raised and red.

Camden's mouth made a sour turn. "Don't care much for tattoos, but the 1911 is a helluva thing. I'm a revolver man myself. Those automatics are sexy, so I see the appeal. But when you absolutely, positively need a gun to work, grab a revolver. Of course, up here, I understand you really don't want to take the chance of a bullet passing through the hull." He stopped talking to look around at the hull of the module, as if imagining a bullet puncturing it.

Then he went on. "So I had my R&D guys fix me up one of these." He reached behind his back and pulled out what looked like a blocky, squarish pistol. But instead of a barrel on the front, it had a flat metal square the size of a stamp. Almost everyone around the table jerked back from the sight. Everyone except Roger, who frowned uncomfortably. Camden went on, "They taught us in the Marines not to go anywhere unarmed." His once faint Texas drawl had become exaggerated. He winked at Roger like a drunk uncle, then held his arm out straight, sighting at an empty wine packet. "It's like a regular stun gun you can buy, but it's got more balls. And I can set it from 'stun' up to 'kill', just like on Star Trek." He leered, then he swung the gun toward Leroy and touched him on the chest with it.

The gun didn't make a sound, but Leroy's head jerked forward and his whole body stiffened. When Camden pulled the gun back, Leroy's eyes were closed and his mouth open, tongue out like a thirsty dog.

"Whoa!" yelled Camden, holding his hands up in mock astonishment. "What the hell, right? Is this guy crazy?" He looked around. Peter, Roger, and Raquel had all pushed backwards from the table until they ran into walls, which, in here, was not far enough for comfort. The module always felt cramped, but now it was suffocatingly claustrophobic. Peter looked rapidly around for something sturdy to shove between himself and Camden. He noticed Raquel deliberately grabbing onto a strap with her left hand, and setting both feet against solid surfaces, literally bracing herself for whatever was about to happen. Roger stared at Camden, not even bothering to stop himself as he slowly floated toward Peter, his face caught somewhere between outrage and curiosity.

Camden's voice lowered as he continued, "No, my brethren, not crazy. Just very determined to do our Lord's will." He paused and looked each of them in the eye in turn. "I have heard a Calling; the Lord has given me a task, and His will be done. The fact that you are still alive means you have a chance to help me Serve. Now let's hear it: who wants to serve the Lord, and who wants to get in my way?"

* * *

Peter and Raquel were silent. Roger screamed, "Jesus, Camden! What are you talking about?"

"Let's not blaspheme in here," said Camden sharply. He turned to face the group. "I bribed Roger to let me bring this little cattle-prod up here. Told him I just didn't feel comfortable without it. I never let him in on the larger plan, but we're going to take down the Hubble." Camden stopped, as if waiting for a reaction.

Raquel hissed at Roger, "You *let* him bring that thing up here?"

"I didn't know he was going to *use* it," Roger half-whispered back.

Camden started again, "We're going to take down the Hubble because God doesn't want it up here. He placed the heavens between us and Him so that we would not look upon His face. And He has made me His instrument to ensure this. So we are going to take the Hubble out." Camden paused again, seeming disappointed there weren't objections, then went on, "To the extent that you all assist me, you can survive this trip just fine. To the extent that you hinder me, I will show no mercy. As you have seen. So I ask you again, who wants to help and who wants to get in the way?"

Roger looked around and then answered, "We don't want to die. What do you want us to do? Just let debris go past us without stopping it, and hit the Hubble?"

"No, Roger," Camden answered. "There's no telling when something big enough to do irreparable damage might come along. It might never happen. No, we're going to use the module's arms to throw something at the Hubble, right into its unprotected innards."

"You mean, like, release something we've already captured, and throw it? That could work," said Roger, nodding agreeably. Anything to stay on Camden's good side.

"Not quite, but you're in the ballpark," answered Camden. "We need something with a lot more mass, since it'll be going fairly slow. I don't want to disable the telescope, I want to destroy it. We're going to throw one of the module's escape pods at it. And according to my math, even that won't be quite enough mass, so it's going to need to be an occupied pod. Fortunately, I've got a volunteer to be the occupant," he said, pointing with his gun at the limp form of Leroy.

The three space garbagemen's faces fell. Obviously the "volunteer" was not likely to survive.

"Roger," Camden ordered, "you put the unconscious dude in an escape pod. And Sweet Tits and Blank Stare," pointing with the gun at Raquel and Peter, "need to strap in and get ready to throw." With that, Camden backed up toward the pods.

The instant Camden turned away from them to find a hand hold, Roger twisted his head to Peter and hissed, "We have to call Ground!"

Camden turned back to them quickly and barked, "Roger! Move! And cut the chit-chat. Nobody needs to be talking but me."

Roger stiffened, and then quickly grabbed Leroy by the back of the shirt and began pulling him toward the pods. To Camden, he asked, "Umm, how long will he be unconscious?"

Camden smiled. "Well, it's not an exact science. When the engineers at my company souped it up for me, all we had to test it on were dogs." He turned the stun gun in front of him to admire both sides. "The best we can guess is a short shot will probably put a human down for fifteen to twenty minutes. Two shots will probably kill you. Why do you ask?"

Roger hesitated, and looked at Peter as if in apology, "Because if Leroy wakes up in the pod and punches the Launch button, there's no telling what might happen. If we're still holding on to it with the arms, the pod could thrust towards us and kill us all."

"Oh, is that all?" Camden asked nonchalantly. "Well let's just fix that right now, shall we?" Camden pushed over toward Roger. When he got there, he grabbed the stun gun in his teeth, and, using both hands, abruptly twisted Leroy's neck much farther than it was designed to go, until his head was pointed almost backwards. The sound was like knuckles cracking, and Peter could see where tendons had snapped beneath the skin.

"Problem solved," Camden said, beaming at the wide-eyed crew. "*Now* he goes in the pod. Roger, if you'll do the honors."

Roger's face was pale, and he stared at Camden, panting. Camden's voice was quiet and calm. "Roger, you can put the body in the pod, or you can take his place." He pointed the stun gun towards Roger. "I've got plenty of battery left."

Roger grabbed Leroy's lifeless body. From the smell it was obvious that someone had shit themselves. Peter had always heard people could do that when they died. But it might just as easily have been Roger. "And you two, strap into the robot arm controls. One closest to the Hubble, and the other closest to the escape pods."

As Roger reached the escape pod, he swung Leroy's limp body around to a stop between himself and Camden and jabbed at a button on the panel next to the pod door. "Control, this is Module 3!"

Camden covered the distance between them like a bird of prey. Leroy's body slowed him down as much as a cardboard cutout might. Roger managed to say, "We've got-" before the stun gun was jammed into the side of his neck. Camden pulled the trigger and Roger's back arched and his arms and legs spasmed. Camden reached out with his other hand and grabbed Roger by the throat. Tiny spheres of blood traced red arcs from Roger's mouth and nose.

Camden let Roger go. "Hmm, sometimes one shot does kill. Now we know," he said, as if settling a long-standing bet.

The panel in the wall beeped, and a tinny voice said, "Module 3?" All eyes turned to the panel. Peter inhaled sharply. If Ground had heard enough of what just happened, they might be able to throw a wrench into Camden's insane operation. The voice came back, "Say again, Module 3. We didn't catch that last transmission."

Camden hesitated for half a second, then jabbed the "Talk" button, "Sorry, Control. Just confirming that we don't need the shuttle back yet. Our tourist has decided to stay another twelve hours."

The voice responded, "Copy that, we saw the request come through already. Congratulations, Module 3."

Camden replied, "Yeah, we're all pretty excited up here, Control. Over and out." Then he pushed Leroy's body into the escape pod, which was also Peter's bunk, and looked over to Peter and Raquel, who sat very still, strapped into the controls. He took a deep breath and said, "Roger made a... disappointing choice, and you see where it got him. I'm going to say that again. Roger chose to oppose me, and so I killed him. You're both smart people. So think about this: I need at least one of you alive to help me finish what I've started."

As he spoke, Camden pulled himself closer, from handhold to handhold, and stopped directly behind them. He placed a hand on Raquel's shoulder, and put his mouth an inch from her ear. "I can tell you which one of you I'd rather spend time alone with." His tongue came out and grazed her ear. She jerked her head away, but his big hand shot up and gripped the back of her head, holding it still. He let out a short grunt of a laugh and let her go, then shifted over behind Peter.

Peter could feel the hot breath on his neck. The control sleeves limited his arm motion like a straitjacket. Camden spoke quietly, but loud enough for Raquel to hear. "What about you, Peter? Surely you can be more helpful than your girlfriend here, right? The one you're too shy to talk to? I see how you watch her. Play your cards right, and I might let you have some alone time with her. After I shock her."

He chuckled to himself. Backing up, he resumed in his

loud, overly-friendly voice, "But I think I could have a good time with either one of you! I have simple tastes. Right now it's anybody's game, so let's see who can be the most cooperative!" He paused and looked expectantly at Peter and Raquel. "Now, what do I do to disconnect the escape pod, without launching it to Earth?" he asked.

Raquel answered immediately, "Flip up the plastic cover to the left of the pod door and hit the little yellow button. The big red button will launch the pod and start the Descent Sequence."

Camden turned his glance to Peter, and asked, "Is that correct, Peter?"

Peter had been about to tell him to hit the red button. That would start the full Emergency Eject cycle and would also trigger a big-time alert in Houston. And Camden probably would have killed him for it. Raquel's choice was better: play along and stay alive. Peter nodded, "Yes."

Camden followed her instructions, and then watched the door seal shut and the pod drift clear of its bay. He turned back to Peter and Raquel. "Now, Raquel, grab the pod with your arms, and hand it off to Peter's arms, so he can throw it into the telescope. And remember," he continued, in a mocking impression of a game show host, "whoever does best gets to go home alive!"

Peter didn't find Camden's grin convincing at all. He was pretty sure none of them would be going home alive. Camden had killed two people without a second's hesitation. Peter and Raquel would probably live exactly as long as they were useful to Camden. If they were going to act against him, it needed to be soon. Peter's chest shivered and his hands were trembling. It felt like the wrong time to make a stand, like he should wait until something happened to tilt the odds in their favor. But they were running out of moments. Every second got them closer to being unnecessary to Camden, and a better chance might never come. He wished for some kind of signal to let him know it was time to act.

Raquel nodded sharply to snap the VR headset down over her face, and began moving her arms. Peter snapped his own headset down and turned to his right. In response, two cameras on the module exterior turned to follow his gaze. In his headset he could see, around the curving outer surface of the module, the ends of the mechanical arms Raquel was controlling. Her right gripper seemed to be pecking at the wrist area of the left arm. In the corner of Peter's screen an instant message popped up, from Raquel:

GUN IN MY BUNK

The message would be visible to anyone looking at his monitor, too. Peter deleted the message and snapped his headset up. He looked up to see if Camden had noticed. Camden hovered a meter away, watching Raquel's screen as her mechanical arms maneuvered the escape pod from the upstream end of the module toward Peter's station.

Peter typed on his own left wrist:

GO GET IT

Then he pulled his arms out of the control sleeves.

"Whoa there, Peter. You better stay put if you don't want to get shocked!" Camden said.

Peter kept unstrapping from the controls, talking rapidly, "When Houston sees we released an escape pod, they're probably going to switch all the controls over to Ground Control. Standard emergency protocol. If you want your plan to work, we need to hard-stop all the communications with Houston. The switches are on that panel right there," he said, pointing to the main communication panel behind Camden. Peter was pretty sure his voice sounded shaky and nervous. He went on anyway. No turning back now. "We need to do it quick. Move out of the way and I'll do it."

"Hold on a-" Camden started, but Peter had already

pushed off with his legs, and was moving quickly toward him. Camden pulled himself to the side to let Peter pass.

As soon as he passed Camden, Peter grabbed a handle on the wall and used it to swing himself around, at the same time curling his legs into a ball. When his feet contacted the wall behind him, he shoved off hard, heading toward the tourist. He kept his arms outstretched, reaching for the stun gun. Camden turned at the noise, bringing the gun around, but Peter was ready, and got both hands around Camden's wrist.

Camden was strong. So strong. He pulled his arm, and Peter, in toward his own chest, and used his other hand to punch at Peter's face. The heel of Camden's hand caught Peter in the jaw, hard. Peter's teeth snapped together. His vision blurred. Camden's huge hand came back to Peter's face, grabbing for his eyes. Peter wouldn't last five more seconds close-in to Camden. So he curled his legs up again and used them to push backwards off Camden's chest with every bit of strength he had, letting go of Camden's arm in the process.

The kick knocked the breath out of Camden and forced him backwards into the arm controls. His head banged against the plastic monitor housing. Camden touched the back of his head and the hand came back bloody. His face showed as much surprise as anger. Military training may have prepared Camden for a lot of combat situations, but Peter's move was something he'd never encountered on earth, something that wouldn't work in full gravity. The kick had pushed Peter all the way to Roger's compartment. Roger's ex-compartment, he thought.

Peter wiped blood from his face, where he'd been scratched around the eyes, and looked past Camden. Raquel had gotten out of her control sleeves and was gliding silently toward the crew pods. Peter needed to keep Camden's attention on himself. He hoped he could stay alive long enough for it to matter. Camden followed Peter's gaze and he hesitated, deciding which of them posed the more immediate threat.

Peter used the momentary distraction to push off toward Camden. Peter hadn't been in a fight since the fourth grade, and the intervening years hadn't made him much tougher. But Peter had spent months in zero-G, and Camden was just learning how to move up here. That might keep Peter alive a little longer, maybe long enough. First-timers launched themselves with their legs and flew like Superman. But long-time techs found that it often made sense to travel feet first, and Peter hoped this was one of those times. He was outmatched in hand-to-hand combat, but in foot-to-hand combat, he might make it a real fight.

Camden turned back to face Peter, and saw only rapidly approaching shoes. He moved the gun forward to shock Peter's left leg, but Peter drew it back and used the momentum to help him kick with his right leg. His foot caught Camden in the elbow and forced the stun gun back. With the gun out of the way, Peter kicked again, this time with a hard blow to Camden's collarbone. The impact twisted the tourist, and he grunted. But Camden quickly recovered, grabbing Peter's thigh and hauling him in, back to the close grappling that the bigger man preferred. Camden brought the stun gun toward Peter's face. Peter shrugged his shoulders and twisted, trying to pull his head in like a box turtle, and the crackling electrode contacted his left triceps instead.

It felt like a horrible combination of the time he'd grabbed the hot exhaust manifold on the lawnmower, and the time he'd gotten hit with an aluminum bat while playing catcher. All the muscles on that side of his body contracted so hard he was sure that tendons were tearing away from bone. A wheezing groan escaped his mouth. Peter tried to wall off the pain, but it overwhelmed him, like an unexpected wave at the beach. His tongue tingled with the metallic taste of electricity, as if he'd licked a nine-volt battery. Or a nine-hundred-volt battery.

With his right arm, he reached for Camden's face, but it was an empty slap. The electric shock had taken all the fight out of Peter. Camden shoved him away and turned back toward Raquel. Peter's head hit hard metal. As he felt blackness sucking him inward, peeling his consciousness away from the insides of his eyes, he wished he could've bought Raquel more time. And then he didn't wish anything.

* * *

Peter woke up to Raquel's smell. She was close, looking into his eyes. He tried to look around but felt dizzy. "Camden?" he mumbled.

She continued looking critically at Peter's eyes, doing some sort of assessment. "I shot him in the shoulder," she said, finally, smirking.

Peter made a more frantic attempt to look around and was met by more dizziness. "Where is he?" he croaked.

"He was still fighting me," Raquel said, "even with two in his shoulder. I figured he was either going to kill me or bleed to death." She paused and smiled her tight, mean smile. The scary one that made her eyes squint. "So I stuffed him in a pod and launched it. If he survives the drop, he can go to jail." She paused to take a long pull from a foil pouch of wine.

"That was pretty ballsy, what you did," she continued. "Going after him unarmed, knowing he was going to light you up." She gave Peter a wine pouch of his own, and her warm hand lingered on his. "Houston called. They're sending the shuttle back. So we've only got about forty minutes to join the three-hundred-mile-high club."

* * * * *

I had the idea of space janitors running around in my head for years. When I read George Saunders' great CivilWarLand in Bad Decline, *I really loved that in all his futuristic scenarios, the people had the same petty office annoyances we all have. When some guys at my actual office started talking about Walmart above-ground pools, this story was born.*

This story also received an Honorable Mention from the Writers of the Future Contest in 2019.

BLACK EYE

Old Mr. Zimmerman came in five minutes early and I pointed him to a treatment chair. His bright eyes scanned the other chairs to make sure we were alone, then he leaned over to whisper that he had brought me a homemade lasagna. Then louder, "And how is Wendy doing? Have they made her a partner yet?"

As usual, I told him that my girlfriend was fine, that since she hadn't passed the bar yet, being made a partner was quite a ways off, and that the lasagna wasn't necessary. And as usual he told me he was going to leave it outside my office door, so I would either have to take it or throw it away, and that Wendy was his favorite technical writing student ever. I think he brought me food partly as a bribe so we'd let him stay in the drug trial, and partly because he saw me as an avatar he wanted to live vicariously through, with the exciting job and the beautiful girlfriend. It's sort of heartwarming. The hundred dollars in cash that he slipped my boss every week did a better job of keeping him in the study.

Once he was in the chair, I stuck the monitor contacts to his chest and strapped the inhaler mask on his face for the telomerase vapor. As I finished the setup, I noticed my boss watching me through the observation window. By the time I went into the control room, he was gone. He had left me a sticky note that said, "See me ASAP." I started the data logging for Mr. Zimmerman's vitals and headed to Dr. Ogden's office.

"Come in, and shut the door." Ogden motioned to a chair and I sat. His collarless golf shirt was just slightly too casual for the office, which was his way of showing us that the rules didn't apply to him. "How is Zimmerman looking?" he asked.

I paused to consider. *How to put this?* "No graying in the eyes yet. He reports less joint pain, but he still moves like he is severely affected. His resting pulse is in the nineties. I'd be surprised if he makes it two more weeks until black-eyes."

Ogden heard what he wanted to hear out of that. "No gray sclera at all so far? That's great. I think we can get approval to extend the study another eight weeks." His eyes drifted up from his screen to check my reaction. "I don't have to tell you how much your full support will be worth for those eight weeks."

In other words, if I didn't turn him in to the CDC for padding the trial, I'd keep getting a share of the kickbacks all the patients in the study were paying. And yes, I knew how much it was worth, to the dollar.

I looked at the ceiling instead of saying something I'd

regret. "If he's gray in two weeks, we need to shut it down. We haven't seen significant delay in the onset of symptoms with the other patients. They're wasting their time and money in here when they should be out enjoying the last months they have."

Ogden gave me his big-eyed sad look while he took a hit from an inhaler mask that was connected to a small unmarked metal canister on his desk. "David, you know as well as I do that if they weren't in here, they'd be at some other clinic, probably one that really is scamming them. Or worse."

"Really scamming them?" I tried to keep my voice under control. "As opposed to what, just barely scamming them? The vapor isn't working. We're giving them false hope."

Ogden seemed offended. "The vapor showed promise! We owe it to science to document its effects, even if it turns out to be less than we hoped. The funding we get by extending the study allows me to continue research." Then the indignant expression was gone, replaced by something more malicious. He crossed his arms in a way that accentuated his biceps. He worked out every day and made sure everyone knew it. "And where will you be without that funding? Out there with the rest of them, hoping somebody finds a cure before you contract it? You know no one who works here has caught it. That's not just chance. Some of the things we're doing here are working."

It was true. Everyone knew somebody who had contracted the syndrome the media called "black-eyes", but it hadn't happened to anyone who worked here. Ogden was trying too many things all at the same time for it to be a rigorous scientific test, but something was working. Maybe the ultra-high air filtration, maybe the radiation shielding. I couldn't deny that I was finding excuses to come into the lab early and stay late. The more time I spent there, the better I felt – the safer I felt.

"What's in the can?" I asked, nodding at the gas cylinder on his desk.

Ogden looked at the tank and didn't answer immediately, smoothing his graying goatee. "It's a different form of telomerase, possibly more bio-available than what we're using in the trial."

"I'll go along with eight more weeks if Zimmerman doesn't turn," I said, and headed back to the control room to check the old man's numbers.

* * *

After the last patient of the day, I finished up my documentation and headed for the door. The clinic was in a converted townhouse in an edgy neighborhood, where we weren't quite sure if the regentrification hipsters were going to totally displace the indigenous criminal element or not. It was easy to tell them apart: the hipsters typically drew cutesy things on their breathing masks, like whiskers or handlebar mustaches. The thugs didn't wear masks, because they were too hard to worry about any punk-ass brain hemorrhaging. The location meant we could have a clinic here without a lot of zoning hurdles, but we still kept the building unmarked, except for the tiniest little "Ogden Clinic" sign on the door. When I got to my car, I found it freshly washed, as it was most days. Another little favor from someone desperate to stay in the trial.

Ogden wasn't straight-up evil, I admitted to myself. He never set out to defraud anyone. But as the outbreak had gotten worse, people began offering him little monetary gifts if he would let them stay in his clinical trials. He really was using the money to continue the research – most of the money anyway; he kept a bit for himself. And he began passing some of it to me once I started asking questions about why we would continue a test once we saw it wasn't working.

By the time I got home, Wendy had the apartment smelling of garlic and olive oil. She surprised me with a hug as I walked in, and kissed my neck. "Tough day?" she asked, fixing my hair. She looked fantastic, and I remembered again how lucky I was to come home to her.

"Not too bad, just long," I answered.

"It's not easy doing what you're doing. I really think you're going to figure it out. What does Dr. Ogden say?" she asked as she turned back to the stove.

"He says I'll probably get a bonus in a few weeks. Maybe we could go on a trip like we talked about?"

"Do you really think it's a good idea to be cooped up on a plane with that many strangers with the outbreak like it is?" she asked.

"I wasn't thinking a plane. It's going to be a pretty big bonus. I was thinking we could take a cruise. On one of those smaller boats, with not a lot of people."

"Wow, that much?" she asked. "Shouldn't that money go toward finding a cure?"

Yes, it should.

"Well, this is a special payment, above what we need for research – for my continued support for the telomerase trial. I guess we could donate it somewhere if you really wanted to," I finished lamely. Now I was lying to Wendy to protect Ogden. No, to keep her from learning that I was complicit with Ogden.

"No, no. I know how hard you're working trying to help the people. You need a vacation, too."

I might not seem so heroic if she knew the bonus was hush money to string people along with false hope. I looked around our apartment that she'd filled with unique, interesting, local paintings and pieces of handmade pottery, and I didn't feel unique or interesting. I felt like the most common thing in the world.

"Oh," she continued, "your mom called and wants to know if we can do dinner tomorrow."

* * *

I put on reasonably nice clothes for dinner at Mom's, and they passed Wendy's inspection. We arrived right on time and were greeted with smiles and hugs. Wendy headed to the kitchen to uncover her homemade bread and help with dinner. I wandered around the house and looked for something to repair so I could feel useful.

Over dinner, the conversation quickly turned to my work. My mother held me with her concerned stare. "Do the masks actually do anything to stop it?"

"We really don't know at this point," I answered, trying not to sound bored. "The virus already lives in all of us, and we can't say for sure what causes it to go haywire. We don't know if the trigger is environmental or some other organism. As far as anyone can say right now, the masks don't hurt, but I don't see any benefit to wearing them unless you're around someone showing symptoms. We've seen cases where a quarter of the people in a certain building get it, and other cases where one guy manifests and nobody around him does."

"Good, because Barbara was wearing one at the club on Wednesday and she looked ridiculous. You remember Barbara, don't you? It was that terrible washed-out green color. Why can't they make them in better colors? I'm not wearing one unless you tell me I should." She nodded to punctuate her decision, and then continued, "Do you really have to be around those people? I think you should have an assistant so you don't have to touch them."

"Mom, we're very careful. When I'm in the treatment room, I wear a full respirator mask and gloves. We haven't had anyone who works at the center show any symptoms.

Our precautions are working."

My mother pursed her lips, not quite mollified by that answer. "How long will it be until you find a cure?"

I sighed. "We have no idea. Right now, we're just trying to manage the symptoms. We've had several patients who came in with the early symptoms, the rapid heartrate and uncontrolled movements, and with our treatments they went five or six months before they transitioned into the full-on syndrome instead of the normal two months. But that's just delaying onset. We haven't shown that we can actually prevent onset. And once they turn that corner, the treatment does nothing. They still go through paranoia to death in twenty-one days."

My mother's eyebrows shot up and I realized I'd revealed too much. "How do you know how long they live?" she asked. "They're supposed to go to the zombie camps once they get the black eyes!"

I nodded as reassuringly as I could. "It's okay. We have authorization to keep specific individuals even after full onset instead of sending them on to the hospice camps. But no one touches them. We don't even go in the room with them. The paranoia makes them way too unpredictable at that point. That's the only time they're likely to attack someone." I realized this last comment wasn't helping calm anyone down, so I changed tacks: "And can you please not use that word? They're not *zombies*. They're people who are dying. Sometimes they do violent things because they're desperate and in pain. It's more like rabies than anything." My mom still looked alarmed, but she was calmer, shaking her head disapprovingly. I tried to bring the discussion to a close. "We're a long way from solving this, and the scope keeps getting larger. This is going to get worse before it gets better." I put my fork down, feeling like I'd given that answer ten thousand times.

Wendy reached out and gave my hand a quick squeeze: "We know you're going to figure it out."

My mom smiled. "Let's talk about something else, then. Wendy, are you still looking for houses?"

I poured myself another glass of wine.

* * *

When I approached the clinic the next day, our office manager, Lyle, was standing on the tiny lawn out front, peering at a newly-broken front window, muttering to himself. Seeing me, he spoke up: "They broke in through the front! Nobody breaks in a front window!"

"Who broke in?" I asked. *The police? FBI? CDC?*

"Thieves. We don't know if they wanted to use the drugs or sell them," he answered. "One of them's still in there."

"What? Who?" But Lyle had turned away to pick up pieces of glass, so I climbed cautiously up the gray concrete stairs to the front door. In the entryway, papers were strewn all over the floor. I heard Ogden yelling and followed his voice to the main treatment room, where I found him standing over a thin man who was dressed in burgundy hospital scrubs. Ogden was holding the front of the man's shirt and shaking him, but gently, maybe for my benefit.

"The idiots didn't even get what they came for," Ogden said over his shoulder, "but they sure did fuck the place up looking for it." He let the limp body slump to the floor and gestured around the room. Furniture was knocked over. A fake plant had been smashed against the far door, perhaps in an attempt to break the lock. Ogden stalked out of the room.

I pulled on gloves and bent over the unconscious figure. He looked to be in his twenties and smelled like he hadn't showered in days. Hollow cheeks flanked a long thin nose. His breathing was rapid. I pulled back an eyelid. The part of his eye that should have been white was a dark, glossy gray, almost black. I immediately scrambled backwards and began peeling off the gloves. He probably had a week to live, maybe two, judging by the evenness of the color.

Ogden came back into the room wearing a full-face respirator. "Masks!" he yelled, handing me one, his voice sounding muffled and buzzy. "Everyone, masks! Whatever they did shut down the air filtration systems." He walked back out, shaking his head, and I followed him as I fumbled to get the respirator on.

"What about this guy?" I asked. "You could've told me he's black-eyes!"

Ogden didn't stop walking and yelled back, "He's unconscious. He's not going to bite you."

Around the corner I saw that the door to the equipment room was open, where the filtration system lived. Inside, several large blower units sat silent. I walked in to look around and didn't see any obvious damage. To the right of the blowers there was a large machine I'd never noticed before. It was mostly covered with a black plastic sheet, leaving only its gray metal base exposed. Thick orange cables connected it to its own electrical box on the wall. It had a barely-perceptible hum, like the big green transformer that was in my front yard as a kid.

Ogden appeared suddenly in the room and put his hand on my shoulder. "Come on, we need to make a decision on this burn-up." He tilted his head in the direction of the unconscious man and began pulling me toward the door.

"What decision? When the cops see his eyes they'll take him to a quarantine hospice."

"I'm not sure we need to involve the police." Ogden's hand on my shoulder squeezed tighter, and I allowed him to pull me out the door. He closed it behind us and motioned to lock it, but the knob and lock had been smashed. He was flustered at not being able to lock the door, and stood there fiddling with it, to no avail.

"What do you mean?" I asked. "Insurance won't cover any of this if we don't file a police report."

"Well, insurance may not be the best answer. Our rates are high to begin with because of our specialty. If we report this, they'll just go higher. Let's talk in my office." He led me into his office and shut the door.

"Jason, what's going on here?" I asked. "Burn-ups broke into our office. We've got one unconscious in the hallway. What do you propose we do, give him a stern talking-to and send him on his way?"

"That's just it: he's unconscious." Leaning forward, Ogden lowered his voice: "What if he were to wake up somewhere else? Wouldn't that be simpler for everyone?" His eyebrows rose into his "let's be reasonable" expression. How was he steering this discussion so that *I* was the unreasonable one?

"What do you have against calling the cops? Is there something else I need to know about here?"

"Something you need to know about?" When Ogden repeated my question back to me, he was usually preparing to say something other than the truth. He looked at my chest and took a hit from the gas cylinder. "Look, the thing about it is, we do a lot of cutting edge research here. If the police come in here snooping around, they will absolutely see some things they don't understand. They could get the wrong idea and we might waste a lot of time explaining ourselves, maybe to prosecutors or news crews."

"Prosecutors? Seriously?" I blurted. "For what? It's starting to sound like we're doing something illegal here." I took a long, slow breath. Ogden was hiding something. Jumping on him was just going to make him defensive and clam up. I slowed down and tried again: "Why don't you tell me specifically what you're worried about and we'll figure this out. All our drug trials are on file with the CDC, I know that." I started to say, "Are *you*," but caught myself. "Are *we* working on anything else that isn't on file yet? Something still in development? Is it your new concoction over here?" I nodded to the unmarked gas cylinder on his desk. "Or is it that machine under the tarp in the equipment room?"

Ogden sighed and looked at his desk. I could sense the smooth-talk generator in his head spooling up. He had a few set scripts that he used, with very minor adaptations for each audience. It was really amazing. Anytime something he said got positive feedback, it got incorporated into his set speeches.

He laid his palms flat on the desk and looked me in the eyes. "David, you know what we do here is very important. I'm trying to avoid costly delays for the whole program." I wasn't getting an answer, I was getting his "for the good of humanity" speech. I stood up and was out the door before he could get up from his chair. I made it all the way to the door of the equipment room before he caught up with me.

Ogden put one hand on the door, holding it closed. In the other hand he held a file folder. He whispered, "David, there's no need to do this. Let's go back to my office."

I didn't move. "What am I going to find under that tarp?"

Whispering harshly, "I'll tell you back in my office. Let's not call unnecessary attention."

My office door was three feet away. "We'll talk in *my* office."

"Fine!" he hissed.

My office was in shambles, but that didn't have anything to do with the break in. Ogden looked around to see who might've seen us go inside, and then shut the door. I didn't sit down, but Ogden moved papers out of a chair and sat.

"What's in the equipment room?" I asked.

"Remember our theory that environmental radiation was weakening the blood-brain barrier, and that was triggering the syndrome?" he asked. I nodded. Now that he needed me on his side, it was, "our theory." He continued: "I started looking at ambient radiation, and most of what we get exposed to comes from space. It's a constant background dose that bombards our bodies all the time, day or night. Our cells have adapted to this constant level of radiation, just like they've adapted to normal temperatures and pressures. So I wondered if I could block any of those particles by using opposing particles, sort of the way noise-cancelling headphones work, as a way of reducing the background radiation that we're exposed to."

"I want to know what is in the equipment room," I said, quiet and reasonable.

He went on as if he hadn't heard me: "Well, electrons are something we can easily generate with the right equipment. I thought if I could broadcast enough electrons, they would annihilate some of the incoming positrons. I was able to build a fairly powerful wide-scatter electron generator from some old equipment."

"What old equipment?" He was really going to make me pull this out of him.

"It was from a university lab. They were doing some electron beam experiments that didn't end up working out."

"What were these failed experiments trying to accomplish?" I prompted.

"I think the military was wondering if this could be used as a weapon," he replied, like this was an ordinary thing one might stumble across. I had no words. I started toward my office door. I needed to see under that tarp. Ogden, quicker this time, jumped up and blocked me, putting both hands on my chest and said, "Let me finish. Please."

I pushed his hands aside but stopped trying to get past him. "I'm listening."

"So, if the body experienced less positrons hitting it, because this machine was wiping a lot of them out, it might be less likely to develop the syndrome," he said. "Now, please keep an open mind about what I'm about to tell you." My mind was just on the verge of exploding, so I wasn't sure where that fell on the open versus closed spectrum. "I wanted to try it out on myself first, but the only place we have enough power for the machine is in the equipment room. And unfortunately... your office is between there and my office..."

"What?" I shrieked. "You mean you've been trying this out on *me*?"

"I've been trying it out on *us*. You've just been getting a higher dose than I have, because you're closer. I understand if you're upset..."

"*If* I'm upset?" I yelled, but Ogden didn't stop talking.

"But hear me out. I would've stopped the second I saw negative effects, but there aren't any negative effects. Look..." and he opened the file he'd brought with him. "This is a compilation of the vital statistics we log from ourselves every week, to make sure we aren't developing the syndrome."

I studied the chart for a minute. It was a graph showing multiple colored lines, almost horizontal, but most trending slightly downward. At the top it said "Combined Effects, Dr. Jason O. and David L." At the bottom were dates, and they started last May.

"This has been going on for nine months?" I asked.

"Yes, and think about those nine months," Ogden snapped back, sounding almost triumphant. "You've lost weight, your resting pulse has gone down, your eyeglass prescription has improved. Improved! Nobody's eyes get better as they age! Your blood pressure is down. At the risk of oversimplifying, with positrons cancelled out, your body thinks it's getting sixteen hours of sleep a day. Everyone else's cells get fresh damage from all kinds of sources every day and they can't repair it all quickly enough. This is a big part of what we call aging. But since your cells are getting less new damage every day, they're able to keep up and even *repair* some old damage. Again, I know how ridiculous this sounds, but the effects on my body are as if I've stopped aging. Your body, getting the higher electron dosage, seems to actually be getting younger. It's not just the lack of positrons. You know what else we have going on in here: the ultra-air filtration and the reduced spectrum lighting. These things are all reducing the damage we get every day. But everyone who works here is getting most of that. Only you and I are getting the electron dosage, and it's the best thing that ever happened to us. It's the best thing that ever happened to anybody, really," he finished, sounding like he'd just realized what a saint he was.

"I see. I should be thanking you for bombarding me with military radiation without my knowledge." I shoveled all the sarcasm I could fit into the words, and then added some more.

"Don't be like that, you know..."

I cut him off: "My blood pressure is down? Fantastic. But what else is going on that we aren't measuring? Have you nuked my internal organs? Am I going to drop dead from multi-organ failure? Am I sterile? These are the kinds of things we can measure and track when the subject consents to be in the study!"

He tried again: "Listen, I understand your reservations" — I snorted at "reservations" but he plowed on — "I really do. If it makes you feel better, I've been doing constant assays on myself. Full blood workups every month. Nothing abnormal." He looked at me hopefully.

"Just so we're clear, you've been doing radiation experiments on me without my knowledge, and now you're asking me to help you commit a crime to cover it up?"

"What crime? I want to remove a trespasser from our building. What's criminal about that?"

"Failure to report black-eyes is a crime, and they don't play around with it! And…" But I stopped. I didn't owe him an explanation of what he was asking. "I'm done here." I stood and crossed to the door, but Ogden leapt up and put both hands back on my chest and forced me into the chair behind my desk. Then his hands were on my upper arms, holding them to my sides. I struggled against him, but his grip was incredible. The position put his face a foot from mine.

"I really can't let you leave like that right now. There's something else that I was hoping I wouldn't have to say," he said. "The people who commissioned the study sent those guys who broke in. They think I'm dragging my feet on giving them the results, so they want all my data."

I stopped struggling for a second, rocked again by the sheer insanity coming out of his mouth. "The CDC sent black-eyes to break in and steal your data?"

"It's not the CDC. It's… I don't know for sure who it is. But they're big and they're… serious. Do you really think Zimmerman and his sad-sack cohorts were paying us $500 a week? These were the guys giving us the cash. And now they've run out of patience. I need to get out of town for a while, and I need you to come with me," he hissed, sounding desperate.

"Why do I need to come with you? I'm not going to let you keep testing me…" I started trying to stand up, but he pressed me back harder.

His face was now inches from mine. "Because, to them, having the test subject is almost as good as having the data. I have reason to believe that you might be immune to the syndrome." He paused and looked at me, waiting for me to prompt him. There was only one reason he'd think I was immune, but I wouldn't say it. He blurted it out, "I've been disabling the filters in your respirator for two months now and you've shown none of the signs of exposure."

No intelligible words came out of my mouth, just grunts, as I tried to wrench my arms free. But I couldn't get loose.

He hurried on, "That's why you need to come with me. You don't understand these people. They'll continue the testing on you and not give you any choice on the matter."

"*You* didn't give me any choice in the matter to begin with. I'm not going with you." With that I jack-knifed forward with all my strength, lowering my head into his chest and driving forward with my legs. Ogden fell backward against my desk.

I was up and surging past him, toward the door, but he caught my shoulder from behind and spun me around. He pressed me against my office wall, his left hand gripping my throat. The space was so cramped I couldn't get away from him. I pried at his fingers while he reached back with his other hand, grabbing for anything and coming up with my desk lamp. As he swung it at my head, I got my arms up to block most of the blow. But this just freed up his other hand to increase the pressure on my throat.

I couldn't breathe. I could hear blood pounding in my ears. My arms flailed at him, but he was too close for a real swing and my punches felt feeble. My vision began to narrow to a small tunnel. Then it went dark.

* * *

I smelled something smoky.

Smoke. My eyes shot open, but I saw only darkness. My head hurt. Most of my body hurt. I was lying on something hard. I tested my arms and legs. They worked, and banged against hard metal when I moved them. And there was smoke. Not pleasant campfire smoke. Burning plastic and metal, like an electrical fire. I attempted to stand up. My head swam; I saw stars, and fell over something, maybe a chair. My ribs ached, and breathing was hard.

Then the noise started, a loud intermittent buzzing. Fire alarm. With that, emergency lights kicked on above me, extremely bright in spots, but not illuminating the small room very well. The weird shadows and angles began to resolve. I was on the floor of my office. I had spent hundreds of hours in this tiny room, but the odd lighting and my novel seating position made it seem completely alien. I rose to my knees and turned my doorknob. The knob turned, but the heavy steel door wouldn't open. I noticed, for what seemed like the first time, that there was a keyed deadbolt above the knob. How could I have never noticed that deadbolt, with a keyhole on the inside? That had to be against fire code. I didn't remember ever getting a key for it, but I checked my pockets automatically. No keys at all. No phone either. In my back pocket I found a strange wallet that held Dr. Jason Ogden's driver's license. These observations were coming in but my brain couldn't put them together. Nothing made sense.

The fire alarm continued its grating buzz, but there was another noise behind me, like a snorting cough. I spun around and saw someone sitting in the chair behind my desk. Slumping more than sitting, head lolled to one side. Dirty hospital scrubs, skinny. It was the kid from the break-in. He wasn't moving. Never mind the fire, I was locked in this little room with a burn-up.

I scanned the room frantically and grabbed the lamp Ogden had hit me with. My blood was smeared on the base. Great, I had an open wound, near a guy with a contagious disease.

I looked back at the door: steel, very thick. Smoke crept under the bottom and spiraled up the heavy steel frame around it. I coughed. The door was warm to the touch. I grabbed the doorknob and yanked with everything I could. Nothing. It was as solid as a bank vault. Not going anywhere.

I looked back at the frame. The hinges were on my side of the door! If I could drive out the hinge pins, I might be able to pull the door off the hinges.

I searched around but knew I didn't have any tools in here. I ended up with a mechanical pencil. I held it at the bottom of the hinge pin and drove the heel of my hand upward into it, gently at first but hitting harder each time. The plastic pencil shattered and the shards punctured my hand. The pain was not terrible, but the amount of blood coming out was alarming. I cursed in surprise and heard an answering yell from behind me.

I whirled to find the burn-up with his shiny dark eyes fully opened. He was still in the chair, pushed back as far against the wall as he could get it. In the dim light his eyes looked completely black. I couldn't even tell which way he was looking. I didn't know what he might do, but he seemed panicked. I put as much calm in my voice as I could muster, which was not much: "We're locked in this office and there's a fire outside. Help me find a way out." He didn't answer at first, but his coal-black eyes got wider.

Then he began yelling, "They told us the cure was in here!" He gasped for air, his voice rasping: "They told us if we broke in and got all the papers and hard drives, the cure for black-eyes was in them. You guys have the cure but you're keeping it secret! Why would you do that?" His gasps were almost sobs.

"We don't have a cure," I said, almost apologetically. "The guy who found a way to slow the spread of the disease is the guy that locked us in this room."

And apparently set the place on fire, I thought.

"I need it for my brother!" With something like a whimper, he picked up my metal garbage can and began slamming it against the wall. I backed up to the door, holding the bloody lamp between us. He continued slamming the can into the wall, but it wasn't in rage. He was doing it methodically, hitting the same spot every time. After a few more hits, he stopped and felt the wall. He had made a dent but not a full hole. He collapsed back into the chair, and almost fell out as it swiveled underneath him.

I picked up the other chair, the one I kept for guests. It was heavy and square and metal, painted beige with a cushion a dead shade of blue only the government would specify. "Let's try this," I said, and began bashing the chair into the same spot he'd been hitting, using one beige leg as my impact point. After several hits, I pierced the drywall and made a hole big enough to put my hand in.

Inside the wall was a perforated steel mesh. It looked like a cheese grater, but thicker and more solid. I hit the chair against it a few times. It bulged outward slightly but I didn't come close to piercing it. I'd never seen anything like it. It must be the extra radiation shielding Ogden had put in the walls when he'd expanded the treatment room six months ago. He told me about it, but I'd never seen how substantial it was.

I turned to see the burn-up doubled over in a coughing fit. The smoke was getting thicker, and the door was so hot I couldn't keep my hand on it. "There's steel reinforcement in the walls. I don't think we can break through it." I'm not sure if he heard me. His breathing was rapid and shallow, and every other inhale ended in a cough. But I wasn't coughing. His metabolism had been accelerated by the disease, causing very rapid respiration. But I had the opposite symptoms: Ogden's experiments had slowed my breathing, thanks to his damn radiation bombarding me all day through the walls. The realization made the hairs on my neck stand up. Radiation, bombarding me through the walls! Ogden wouldn't want radiation shielding between me and his machine, would he?

"Move!" I ran around my desk, carrying the chair. The startled burn-up scrambled out of my way. "We need to move this desk. I think there won't be any of the metal shielding in the wall toward the equipment room."

Ogden must have gotten my desk and my chair at the same auction. It was old and steel and weighed a ton. We heaved together and shifted it a few feet, enough for me to get a good swing at the wall. The effort was too much for the kid; he began coughing, slumped against the desk, and slid to the floor.

I couldn't stop to check on him. The room was getting hotter, and the smoke made it hard to see, not to mention breathe. I swung the chair at the wall and it made a dent. I swung again and made a hole big enough to get my hand in. I reached in and felt the paper backing of wallboard on the other side. I began tearing out the sheetrock on my side of the wall. It wasn't easy: the institutional wallpaper in here was sturdy stuff, almost like fabric. Once I tore a good sized chunk away, I could see I wasn't going to be able to break a very big hole through here, just the width between two wall studs. Maybe sixteen inches wide if I was lucky.

I tore more sheetrock out. I had enough space now that I could swing the chair and hit the sheetrock on the other side. Three swings and I had a small hole, but breathing was getting tougher. I enlarged the hole and stuck my head through. The equipment room looked about the same as my office: dark and smoky. I pushed with my shoulders until the wallboard broke and I tumbled through onto the floor. The lock on this door had been smashed, and the door swung open easily.

Outside in the main room, flames were everywhere, consuming the furniture and licking up the walls. The smoke was so thick that if I didn't know the layout by heart I wouldn't know which way to go.

I heard a ripping noise above me and jumped back as a chunk of flaming ceiling fell. I had very little time. Getting out was going to be tough. Maybe impossible if I had to carry a burn-up. I could see the front door from here. The kid had two weeks to live, best case. What would Ogden do? He'd save himself. Could I explain to Wendy that I left a kid to die?

I went back into the equipment room and crawled back through the hole in the wall into my office. The black-eyes was still on the floor, not moving. I felt his pulse, and it was faster than I could easily count. I dragged him to the wall and realized that I was never going to be able to push him through the hole. If I'd been thinking of getting him through it, I'd have made the hole lower to the ground. Maybe next time. I ran my knuckle down his breastbone to wake him. He grunted. I did it again and his hand came up to stop me. "Hey…" I yelled. I couldn't call him "black-eyes." I tried again, "What's your name?"

"Steven," he wheezed out, and opened his eyes. "But people call me Chug."

"Steven, I'm David. We're getting out through that hole in the wall, but you have to help me."

He made an effort to sit up and I guided him to the hole. He got his arms through, and I pushed his butt until he flopped onto the floor on the other side. I clambered through right behind him, not waiting for him to move out of the way. I grabbed him around the waist. From the front of the building I could hear sirens, and we stumbled toward them. My eyes watered and my throat was raw from the smoke.

Steven slumped to the ground, so I dragged him behind me through the narrow front hallway, holding him under the arms. I tripped over one of our respirator masks on the floor, picked it up and put it on before continuing. It made the gasping breaths I was taking slightly less painful.

I made it to the front door. Fortunately, Steven and his companions had helped us here too by smashing the lock, and the door stood slightly ajar. I kicked it open and felt the cool air on my wet skin. I pulled Steven out of the doorway.

In movies, the firemen come striding out of the building carrying people in their arms. I was dragging a very skinny guy across the ground and it was almost more than I could manage. He looked up at me and smiled. A few people stood across the street watching, filming with their phones. I could see flashing blue and red lights coming down the street.

Steven called out, "David..." I bent down to hear him. "When the cops get here, they're going to take me away. They'll put me in a black-eyes camp and..."

I cut him off, "Go now. Run. They haven't seen you yet."

"I can't run," he wheezed. "I can't even stand. I don't care about that. I want you to find my brother and put him in your trials. Please. Will you do that? We were sharing a bedroom when my eyes started turning. He needs it." He pulled a pen from his back pocket and wrote a name and address on my hand. "Will you do it? Please? He hasn't done anything wrong. He doesn't deserve this." He gestured at himself.

I looked in his shiny black eyes and nodded.

* * *

It'll take a few more months to fully repair all the fire damage, but we were able to let patients back in just a week after the firemen left.

Yesterday we mounted the new sign out front. Nobody wanted the clinic to stay named after Ogden, and I didn't want it named after me, so we named it after the guy who made us re-examine how we operate. It reads: "Steven 'Chug' Dawson Memorial Clinic." Ogden can object if he ever shows back up. So far we haven't heard anything from Ogden, but we haven't heard from his shadowy funders either. I guess that means that *they* found Ogden.

Steven's brother works the reception desk when he's not being treated himself. He has that same thin nose as his brother, but without the sunken cheeks. He grins as he lets Mr. Zimmerman in, who looks at least ten years younger.

Even after I explained the risks to them, neither of them could wait to try the electron generator treatment. With that and Ogden's last version of the telomerase vapor, we're actually starting to make some progress on the syndrome.

And Mr. Zimmerman insists he needs his strength if he's going to make all those lasagnas for my wedding.

* * * * *

Driving to work in 2014, I had the germ of the idea for this story. What if you worked at a place doing medical experiments, but they were also doing experiments on you? The black-eyes disease was what I came up with as the main mission for the clinic. I liked the idea that it was a deadly disease, but that a zombie-obsessed public would perceive it as zombie-ism. I feel like there are more stories to tell in this particular world.

Project Never

Dear Stephanie,

I know there's not much point writing all this. You're not going to believe it. Trust me, I know how crazy it sounds. But I have to tell you. In the reality I come from, you died in 2023. You were hit by a car.

It happened on a Thursday, April 11th. I was at work. The police called me and told me. You'd been on the east side of Manhattan, shopping I guess, and a human-driven car swerved onto the sidewalk, hit you, and kept going. They never caught the driver.

I saw you at Bellevue, but it wasn't much of you in there. A mangled inflated thing, with tubes in it. This is the image that tainted all my good memories of you. When they tell kids not to look at the body in the casket, but to remember how the person looked alive, this is why.

I fell apart. I was a zombie all through the funeral. Your mother made most of the arrangements. She was thoughtful, but I think she sort of blamed me. Like if it weren't for me you wouldn't have been in New York in the first place, and now look what happened.

I spent the next few months trying to figure out what to do with your ashes. I thought about taking them to one of the places we'd always talked about going, Hawaii or Sweden or somewhere. It tore me apart to think about all the things we never got around to doing. With my job, and the thousand little sacrifices and commitments we made for family and friends, we just never made the time. In the end, you just sat on the dresser in the bedroom.

I started spending a lot more time at work, because when I got home you weren't there. There was nobody to listen to me rant about my job. Nobody to gently mock me, or give me your inexplicably optimistic take on the day's events. There was nothing to do but drink and relive every fight we had — every time I ignored you, every time you threatened to leave. It was right around the time that all the big landmarks were getting attacked: the St. Louis Arch, the Washington Monument. But you wouldn't know that. All that happened after... Anyway, as busy as it was at Homeland, I could log all the overtime I wanted and nobody mentioned it. So I stayed late most nights, translating innocuous intercepted phone calls between people whose main transgression was speaking another language.

Our friends kept inviting me to hang out, but it was too weird, everyone tiptoeing around the lack of you, not sure if they were supposed to apologize that you were gone, or pretend that you never existed.

* * *

It was almost two years after it happened when the ugly guy knocked on our door. Short, thin and fit, with thinning hair. He was mostly forgettable, except that his face was not good to look at. He turned up right after I got home from work, before I'd even got a beer opened.

"Allen D'auria?" he said. No greeting, he just led with my name.

"Yes, can I help you?"

"I'm Morris Peters, Mr. D'auria." He held out official-looking DARPA credentials that said the same thing. "I'm with Defense Advanced Research Projects. I'd like to speak with you about a job. Do you think we could talk inside?" He stood there actually waiting for me to invite him in.

"I, uh, sure, I guess..." I led the way to the living room, then grabbed a beer from the fridge and asked if he wanted anything. He didn't, and I said, "Are you sure you got the right Allen D'auria? I mean, you guys design weapons, right? I'm a linguist. Arabic languages."

He smiled, leaning across the kitchen counter. "I don't mind telling you, Mr. D'auria, we've had our eye on you for quite a while as you've risen through the ranks at Homeland. You're the right one. Yes, we do design weapons, and test them and deploy them, among a lot of other stuff. And right now we could really use a few guys like you."

When he turned to look around the place, I figured out that it was his total lack of a chin that made him so unfortunate looking. From the side, it was like one smooth curve from his nose down to his Adam's apple. It made his otherwise unremarkable nose protrude like a beak.

"One of our projects is focused on preventing domestic terrorism," he said. "We have a special operations team that is very capable tactically, but we fall short on getting close to the subjects. We don't speak the language and we don't look the part." He cleared his throat and looked at the floor. "We were made aware of the loss of your wife... I'm very sorry."

I nodded in acknowledgment. I didn't really need the reminder of the anniversary coming up.

"We know you've been really throwing yourself into your work," he continued, barely stopping to breathe. "We think you might appreciate the chance to get a little closer to the action. Your language skills and olive complexion will help us bridge that gap. Our special ops guys will work with you and get you ready for field work. That is, if you're interested..."

I was pretty stunned. Everybody at Homeland Security — hell, everybody involved in the War For Freedom — thought about field work. Those were the sexy jobs, the stuff they make movies about. But those guys usually either came from the military or started very young. You didn't just go into field work after fifteen years at a desk.

He watched my eyes and started talking again like he could read my mind. "I understand field work is not your background. But believe me, our guys are top tier, and they will make you top tier. In fact, more than anything, that would be your job for the first several months: training, working out, and learning all the James Bond stuff that the CIA guys know. It's really the chance of a lifetime."

I was interested. Hell, I was flattered. "That sounds attractive," I started. Really attractive compared to ending up an obese corpse in my cubicle. "But, uh... what exactly is the job?"

He chuckled. "Okay, well, here's the thing," he said, the faint trace of a Boston accent showing up as he relaxed. "I'm not joking about how top secret this is, so I can only give you vague answers. If you back out, we can't have you knowing too much. What we do dovetails very closely with what you do now. We surveil the bad guys and look out for danger signs. The difference is, instead of just handing that intel off to someone else, we're authorized to actually move in and stop them. And we have some cutting-edge tools to do it with."

He straightened and took a deep breath. "Look, this is a big ask, and you don't know me. Why don't we set up a visit for Saturday? Again, I can't reveal too much, but you'll see that we are who we say we are, and that we're serious."

I hesitated; this was a lot to take in, and very quickly. But where was the harm in talking to the guy? Honestly, with the anniversary of your accident coming up, any distraction was a welcome one. "This Saturday?" I asked, like a had a packed social calendar. "Yeah, I can do that."

Morris smiled. "I thought you'd be interested. I'll pick you up here at ten, okay? Dress like you're going for a hike." He walked to the door and went out, calling back over his shoulder, "You won't regret this."

* * *

Saturday snuck up on me after a few late nights at work. Dress like I'm going for a hike? What the hell was that supposed to mean? I stood in the closet wondering when was the last time I went on a hike. That time you dragged me to the Catskills for somebody's wedding? I put on jeans and was tying those New Balance running shoes you bought me when we decided we were going to start exercising, when the doorbell rang. Morris stood there in pants that had a lot of zippers, and a fleece vest. I think he hiked more often than me. He ushered me into a brown Toyota Camry and we headed uptown.

"I thought the government had to drive American brand cars?"

Morris glanced over at me as he drove. "Yeah, that's the policy. But we're allowed to bend the rules quite a bit. Being able to blend in with the landscape is a lot more important than selling a couple more domestic cars."

We parked under a glass and steel office building uptown and took an elevator up. Morris had to put his ID in to access the 8th floor, where we emerged into a bright empty hallway with a few doors down its length. Morris swiped his ID at the first door and we went into a large room full of black computer monitors.

"I asked the guys to step out for a minute," Morris said. "So you could look around without seeing anybody's face."

He moved a mouse and several monitors lit up. Two were surveillance camera views: an exterior of a building and an interior of a room. In the room, a guy sat on a couch playing a video game. The third screen was scrolling text. Every time the guy swore in Arabic at the Xbox game, his words marched across the other screen in English.

"This is a little beyond what you've got at Homeland, I know."

Yeah, a little. Our setup looked like a LeapPad compared to this. This was *CSI: Mars* stuff here.

"We spend a lot of time just watching and listening. But we always have to be ready to jump in and disrupt. So we wanted to let you tag along with a team on a training run."

I followed Morris back to the elevator and we travelled up with another swipe of his ID. We came out on the roof, where a helicopter sat idling. "Not scared of heights, are you?" he called over the thumpy whine of the engine.

He opened the door of the chopper that was marked KFOL News and motioned for me to get in. In the back sat two very military-looking guys, wrapped in muscles and tactical clothes and gear, with black automatic pistols strapped to each leg. Their faces were hidden by balaclavas and sunglasses. Morris and I packed into the cramped space, which showed no signs of any cameras or newscasting gear. The nearest soldier reached a hand out. "Good to meet you, Allen. I think you're going to enjoy this."

I shook his hand and nodded mutely.

The chopper lifted off and we headed north. Once we left the city, we kept alarmingly close to the ground, moving fast. The motion was stomach churning, like that rollercoaster in San Antonio that made me puke. You would've loved it. Twenty minutes later, we were past land and over open water. The chopper slowed to a hover and Morris took off his vest, revealing his own gun in a shoulder holster.

"THE BIRD WILL TAKE YOU TO SHORE," Morris shouted. "WE'LL MEET YOU THERE IN TEN!"

He held out all his fingers as a visual aid. Then one of the soldiers opened the door and just stepped out, like we might be sitting on solid ground. The other soldier followed, and then with a wave to me, so did Morris. I leaned over after him and watched as he fell feet-first into the dark gray water thirty feet below.

I sat back, suddenly alone in the back of a helicopter, wondering what kind of fucked up job interview this was. I wasn't sure what to do, until the pilot loudly told me: "SHUT THAT DOOR!" Before I could comply, the chopper pitched violently back towards land, and I reached out awkwardly and slammed the door.

The pilot set down on a gravelly swath of what passed for a beach up here in what must be eastern Connecticut. I got out and the chopper left me there. There were no people and no buildings, just tall yellow grass whipping in the chilly wind. I stood there imagining how cold that water must be. I didn't see signs of anyone swimming until the first man was very close to shore. He came on land low, almost crawling, scanned his surroundings, then spat a rubber mouthpiece out and let it dangle by a tube that ran down his neck.

"Tiny air tank," he said, noticing my curious look. "Let's us do the last fifty meters underwater for extra sneakiness." He smiled at this while he pulled the balaclava up over the dark skin of his face. The other two men came onto the shore, doing the same low walk until they reached me, and then stood. They were dripping wet, and must've been freezing, but they didn't show it.

Morris grinned at me. "I'm not just a recruiter, I'm also a member," he said, slightly out of breath. "These guys are the real badasses, but I try to keep up." Turning to the man who had come out first, he said, "Alpha, you want to brief our man?"

The tall man, Alpha, turned to me. "Just over that hill is a house with some bad guys in it. We need to go in fast and neutralize between two and four subjects. They will probably be armed, but they should not be expecting us." He pulled the big automatic pistol from his left leg and handed it to me, grip first. "Here, you can take my spare. It's all about redundancies and back-up plans. Never bring one gun if you can bring two." Seeing my look of apprehension, he drew the right-side pistol, pointed it at Morris, and fired.

"Shit!" Morris yelled, his hand going to his butt and coming away with bright pink dye on it.

Alpha looked back to me, continuing to hold out the back-up gun: "Simunition rounds. This is just a training exercise." I accepted the gun from him, holding it gingerly like it might go off at the slightest bump. Alpha turned to Morris and chuckled: "That was for being last on the beach."

Morris was still rubbing the dyed spot, and smiled ruefully. "Remember who's got your back, jackass."

Morris pulled me aside from the others and fixed me with a focused look. "Listen, this is a big part of the screening. We don't really arrest people, okay? We disrupt plots. Can you kill an enemy of our country?" He paused while I was busy not answering him. "The guys who come to us from the military," he went on, tilting his head toward Alpha, "they already answered this question when they enlisted. But you've never really been asked, am I right?"

I nodded my head in agreement. For fifteen years I'd watched potential criminals. And listened. And betrayed their secrets. But I never killed anyone. Punishment was somebody else's thing.

"Look, they're not 'suspects.' There's no question of innocence or guilt. We take down bad people at exactly the right time. Can you pull the trigger?"

I took a slow deep breath and thought about it. I thought about how the military kills people in battle, without a trial. I wondered if that was something I could do. The image of someone lying dead on a battlefield reminded me of you, dead on the sidewalk. I hadn't been there, but I'd imagined what it must've looked like thousands of times. I thought about the guy who ran you over and just drove away, and I decided that yes, some people deserved to die.

I nodded. "Yeah, I think I can."

"Okay, then let's see," Morris said, turning back to Alpha and giving him a thumbs-up.

Alpha started walking inland, bent low at the waist. "Follow my lead: Allen to my left, Beta to my right, Morris to the rear."

We all crouched and walked with him into knee-high yellow grass. I tried to copy his stance, gun held out in front with both hands, pointed at the ground, head constantly scanning from side to side. It occurred to me that I didn't know if the gun was cocked or if the safety was on, or if it even had one. But it didn't seem like a convenient time to ask.

When we crested the hill, I saw a small rundown wooden building the size of a house. From the flagpole and parking area, I got the idea it might have been an old state park ranger station. Alpha gave a complicated hand-signal to Beta, which apparently meant to sweep around the right side of the building. To me, he patted his left leg and pointed forward with his hand flat. I guessed that meant stay with him. I looked back and saw that Morris had dropped to the ground in the tall grass behind us, a revolver in his hand, and his head scanning left and right.

The one called Alpha crept to the front door and tried the knob. Reaching into one of the many pockets on his vest, he pulled out some kind of black metal lock-picking device, and within twenty seconds he was quietly pushing the door open.

He stepped through the doorway low and fast, sweeping the room with his gun in front. I followed, trying not to make any noise. I kept telling myself this was just an exercise, but the adrenalin was in full force, pulse pounding in my temples, waiting for someone to jump out at us.

The room was empty except for dirty brown furniture. Alpha made a bunch of hand signals that were lost on me, and then walked purposefully across the room. He was halfway through the far door when I heard gunshots from his direction. I didn't know if it was Alpha firing or someone else, but there were flashes and bangs. The noise was physically painful, like sudden sharp stabs on both sides of my head. With the overwhelming sounds and the quick flashes and smoke from gunshots, I was terrifyingly disoriented. All I could see was Alpha's back ahead of me. Then I was aware of movement in a doorway to my left. A small man rushed into the room carrying a rifle. He took a second to scan the room, and focused not on me, but on Alpha and all the commotion coming from his direction. My arms automatically swung the heavy pistol up toward the newcomer. As he brought the rifle to bear on Alpha, I had an instant of panic: Alpha had showed me that *his* gun fired simulation rounds, but what about mine? Did I have real bullets? Was this the actual test?

It was too late, my finger was already squeezing the trigger. The muzzle flashed and the gun jumped in my hand.

The interloper jerked back and I saw bright orange dye erupt on his chest. He staggered sideways and looked up at me, apparently noticing me for the first time. His mouth twisted into a smirk as he laid the rifle down, and then lay down on the ground next to it.

I couldn't see Alpha anymore, but the popping of shots continued in his direction for a few seconds. After the shooting stopped, Alpha came walking back in the room, yelling, "Stand down! Threat is neutralized!" He looked down at the man on the ground, then up at me. Alpha's face was still hidden behind the mask, but I was pretty sure he was smiling as he nodded and gave me a thumbs-up.

* * *

Two days later Morris called me and I took the job. You know me, I like a clean break. There was nothing for me in New York but ghosts of you. If I walked past Buona Notte, I remembered you drinking too much Chianti and trying to sing. Anywhere near Grand Central, I remembered the waiters singing you *Happy Birthday* at the Oyster Bar, and how mad you got. It was like that all over the city. So I didn't argue when they told me I'd be moving to the headquarters in Chicago.

Their building there was imposing, an old manufacturing plant or something, built way back when you wanted your factory to look like a cathedral. Rolling lawns like a golf course led right up to the main structure, that was all dark stone and spires, and absurdly tall doors. Morris met me at the doors and walked me past the very understated DARPA sign, past receptionists, then left through heavy unmarked steel doors, to a gym. He hadn't got any better looking.

"Throw your stuff in a locker," Morris said. "Andre, well, you know him as Alpha, should be here in a minute." Just then Andre came in from another door, covered in sweat. Without all his gear he looked just as military. Shaved head, lined face, ramrod posture, and not an ounce of fat on him. He smiled and stuck out his hand.

"Glad to have you aboard, Allen. Step one is to get you in shape. I'll give you a tour, but we're going to do it running." We took off through the building. Andre would sprint for forty-five seconds, with me struggling to keep up, and then walk fast for fifteen seconds while he pointed things out to me. "Pool... firing range through there, training room and classrooms over that way." When we reached the back to the building, we went out the door and onto a paved trail that wound through woods. He kept up his sprint-and-walk routine here too. "High intensity interval training is the fastest way to get in shape. We'll usually start the day either out here or in the pool. Then classroom, then weights. Then lunch. Then more of the same." He laughed, and took off again. "Try to keep up so I don't lose you."

I would've yelled some clever answer after him, but I was breathing too hard.

From that day on, we ran, we swam, we did push-ups and pull-ups and obstacle courses. It was just like the boot camp scenes you see in the movies, except instead of a platoon of young recruits, it was just middle-aged me. And instead of some angry drill sergeant calling me a worthless maggot, I had Andre yelling, "You got this! It's all you! One more rep!" like we were long-time gym buddies.

Beta's name turned out to be Phil. He worked out with us, and taught me basic and then advanced first aid. "If a guy gets hurt, any one of us is trained to help him. Gotta learn how to fix people before we learn how to break 'em."

I probably lost ten pounds over the next two months. I didn't see much of Morris after the first day. They set me up in a little apartment near Wicker Park, but I didn't see much of that either. We trained all day. They taught me how to fight. I learned how to shoot like a sniper, how to scuba dive like a SEAL, and how to drive like a stuntman.

There were about ten other guys I saw irregularly. Some would sit in on special classes I was taking, some would train with us for a few days at a time. But mostly it was just me and Andre and Phil. I started eating all my meals at the HQ, and by the time I got back to the apartment, all I could do was crawl into bed.

On Tuesday of the ninth week, Morris was waiting for us when we got out of the pool. He looked me up and down, then said, "New stuff to see today." After I changed, he led me past the receptionist, this time to the unmarked metal doors to the right of the entrance, doors I'd never been through. "Your card will work here now." He indicated a security box next to the door. I held my ID up and heard a buzz. Morris pulled the door open. Inside was a long hall with doors on either side. There was a whiteboard to the left, and someone had written in huge red letters: "PROJECT NEVER."

We walked down the hall, passing the open doors of offices. Two of them had the same surveillance setup Morris had shown me in New York. "Andre says you're doing great," Morris continued. "I'm going to tell him to ease up on you before you start looking too much like him. Andre is a fantastic operator, but he's not much use undercover."

As he led me through the third door on the right, he kept up his monologue. "All that stuff you've been learning is pretty standard Special Ops stuff. Today you get to see what we do that no one else does." We were in a large, dim room. The far wall was all glass, thirty feet wide. Two guys in jeans and collared shirts sat at desks along the wall to the right, their computer screens full of text. It looked like they were coding, but in no computer language I'd ever seen. On the other side of the glass wall was what I imagined a wind tunnel built by high school kids would look like. It was basically tube shaped, open at both ends, about twenty feet long and ten feet wide and tall, all covered in dull gray metallic foil. There were thick cables plugged into it every foot or so, and cameras pointed at it from several angles.

Morris motioned to the programmers: "This is Bill and Karl." As they turned to us, Morris indicated me, "And this is Allen, who I was telling you about. The new linguist. You want to give him the show?"

Bill stood up. He was stocky and had his hair tied back in a short ponytail. He grinned as he asked, "Have you told him anything about it?"

Morris shook his head. "Not a word. Didn't want to ruin your punchline."

Bill turned to me: "How much do you know about subatomic particle dynamics?"

I was totally unprepared for that one and felt a little ambushed. But everyone was relaxed and smiling, and I remembered how Morris had introduced me. "Well, just as much as I had to know to get a degree in Middle-Eastern languages."

Bill laughed. "It's cool. Just means my explanation can be shorter." He pointed to the tunnel thing behind the glass. "So Verhagen found out that if you get multiple streams of exotic hadrons moving opposite directions past each other, the shearing force between them can create a volume where Newtonian physics gets bent."

The other programmer, Karl, swiveled his chair around to watch our exchange. He was thin and wore big black-framed glasses.

Bill gestured toward the gray tunnel. "If we introduce an object into that volume at a high enough velocity, it is not subject to the temporal arrow." He stopped and looked at me, eyebrows raised. When I said nothing, he went on: "You're kind of expected to call 'bullshit' at this point," he said, the patient smile not wavering.

"I, uh, don't feel like I understand that well enough to call BS. When you say 'temporal arrow,' are you saying you've got, like, suspended animation?"

Morris cut in: "Better. They built a time machine."

Both coders scowled at Morris like he had indeed ruined their punchline. I looked at him to see if he was serious.

"He's not joking," said Bill. He held up a metal cylinder, about a foot long. It looked like a relay baton. "This is our little parlor trick. It's really expensive to do this, but you won't believe us until you see it." He took out a rotary engraving tool and started scratching the cylinder with it. "I'm writing today's date on this. Now I want you to come over and scratch something random on it. Put your first dog's name on it or something. Anything."

I took the buzzing tool and tried to write "Obie" with it. It was frustrating because the spinning tip wanted to drag my letters to the right. The bottom of my "b" scrawled off below the rest of the letters.

"Good. It's fine. The messier the better, really," Bill said. Karl was back at his computer, typing furiously. Bill said, "Okay, now look in the fridge over there." He pointed to the side of the room. I went over and opened the door of the brown dorm refrigerator. It was mostly empty except for energy drinks and a bunch of fast food condiment packs. "Any aluminum cylinders in there?" I looked around again and shook my head.

A low hum started, so low I could feel it in my chest. Morris said, "They just turned on the tunnel, I hope you don't have a pacemaker," his eyes wide with mock concern. "I'm kidding. We know you don't have a pacemaker. Our screening process is very thorough."

Bill walked over to the opposite side of the room. There, in the dark corner to the right of the huge window, a short white tube stuck out of the wall, about chest high. Looking through the glass, I saw that the tube extended a few feet into the next room, and was pointed at the center of the big tunnel. There were plastic hoses running from the tube to a tall tank of compressed nitrogen. Bill stuck our aluminum cylinder into the open end of the tube. "Your dog's name was Obie?"

"Yeah," I said. "We had just seen *Star Wars* when we got him."

Bill turned to Karl and asked, "Go?"

Karl nodded and replied, "Good to go."

Bill stepped on a pedal on the floor and there was a pneumatic *shoop* sound, like a bank transport tube. I saw a blur of motion through the glass at the far end of the tube, then nothing. Everyone in the room turned to watch me now, as Bill said, "Okay, check the fridge again for me."

I obediently turned back to it. In my mind I saw myself opening the door to a still-empty fridge and everyone laughing at me for being so gullible. My hand hesitated at the door handle, but I went ahead and opened it. Lying on the middle rack was the metal cylinder. I picked it up. It was cold to the touch. Next to the date it said, "Obie," still as poorly written as it was two minutes ago.

Bill said, "It ought to be pretty cold. It's been in there for an hour now."

I looked around the refrigerator for some way a foot-long cylinder could get in there. Morris said to the other guys, "One day we should put that fridge up on a table so you can see under it too."

"Whoa," I said, sounding as clever as usual. "What just happened?"

Karl answered, his voice as dry as a textbook: "The cylinder got shot into the non-temporal zone and came out in the refrigerator an hour ago." After reading the look on my face, he added, "Really."

Bill cut in: "So Verhagen figured out the time-shift trick two years ago. And the first thing they found out was that sending something back in time isn't the trickiest part. The tricky part is that the Earth is not in the same point in space as it was an hour ago. It's rotating, and at the same time orbiting the sun, and moving within the galaxy, and it just goes on and on. For a short jump like one hour, we can be very positionally accurate and hit the inside of a refrigerator. If you want to jump back four years, the error in calculating the Earth's position gets bigger, and we're happy to get within twenty meters of the target."

Was I really looking at a time machine? My mouth hung open like I might say something, but nothing came out.

"Look, we know it's a lot to process," Morris said, like he was talking to a five-year-old. "Go home and think about it. You'll have a thousand questions in the morning. Like what it would've looked like if the refrigerator door was open. Or what would happen if you'd got it out of the fridge before we put it in the tunnel."

I nodded like an idiot.

"Oh, and this is just the desktop model," Bill said, indicating the tunnel thing. "The Big Buddy is underneath us."

* * *

I took his advice and went home early. It was only Tuesday, but I went ahead and drank my Saturday beer. Why the hell not? Then I surfed the TV channels, vaguely hoping to find *Back to the Future*, but not *Terminator*. What does a secret government agency do with a time machine? Send a bomb back to kill Hitler? Whatever I thought the answer to that might be, why hadn't they already done it in the last two years? Or had they? How would I know? I'd heard people who experienced earthquakes say they felt unsettled for months, because they now knew the Earth could move at any time. I felt kind of like that. When I finally fell asleep, I dreamed about being back in high school, but I was thirty-seven.

The next day I did, in fact, have a thousand questions. I kept my mouth shut through the morning workout. But after lunch when I got back into the hall of Project Never, I couldn't wait to get them out.

Bill and Karl were still in the room where I'd left them yesterday. Bill smiled. "The answer to your first question is, 'Yes, living things can go through it.' We started out with a mouse, then dogs. They don't like it. They throw up. A lot. And the radiation's certainly not good for them. But they live."

"No," said Karl, obviously having played this game before, "the answer to his first question is: 'No, we haven't figured out how to jump forward, only back.' Anybody we send back gets a one-way ticket."

I thought about that for a minute. "Maybe that should have been my first question, but I still want to know what it would've looked like if the fridge had been open."

"Oh. It's not that impressive," said Bill. "The cylinder just pops into existence. No flash of lightning or crazy noises or anything you wish would happen. From a physics perspective, it's actually just sliding into place, but from a direction you can't see..." Bill stopped mid-sentence at the sound of a slight buzzing noise. He hissed to Karl, "Verhagen!" and then to me, while he straightened his shirt: "Dr. Verhagen's coming, the guy who invented this thing."

The buzzing turned out to be a pair of small drones that flew into the room seconds later, each with multiple cameras sweeping the room. They took up positions in opposite corners of the ceiling. They were followed by a tall thin man with unruly curly gray hair and Harry Potter round glasses.

"You must be the new man. Allen, is it?" He shook my

hand and looked at me with the most intense interest.

"Yes, sir," I found myself answering. I hadn't intended to call him "sir." Verhagen just seemed to warrant it.

"I hear good things about you. I understand we just revealed our big secret to you."

"That's right, sir. It's really, uh... incredible." It seemed like an insulting understatement.

Verhagen narrowed his eyes and gave a mirthless smile. "Well, I'm sure Bill and Karl can answer any questions you have. I'll leave you to it." He pivoted and left, the drones sweeping out ahead of him. Both programmers visibly relaxed their posture when he left.

"What's with the drones?" I asked.

"One drone is security," said Karl. "It watches for threats and sniffs for explosives. The other one videos him in case he says something historic."

Bill sighed. "The guy's a genius, no question. But every time you talk to him, it's like he's waiting for you to screw up so he can call you on it."

I nodded in sympathy. "But he invented this... tunnel thing?"

"Yeah, he did a lot of the preliminary work while he was a professor at NYU. Once he was sure what he had, they say he took it to a congressman he knew, and here we are." Bill sat back down, and added over his shoulder, "That congressman is now President Everett."

I thought about it all. "So, what do we do with this tunnel thing?"

Bill smiled and looked over his shoulder at Karl. "Well, I jumped back yesterday, and now I'm Karl's dad..."

"Fuck you," Karl answered around a laugh.

"Seriously, it's a peculiar thing," Bill said to me. "If we send someone back in time, and he changes something in the past, that person has lived through the event the old way, and then the new way, and he can remember it both ways. But for everyone else, we only remember it the new way, because the other way never happened anymore. So we're never quite sure what we've done. There are rumors that there were other, larger, terrorist attacks a few years after 9/11, but that we went back and prevented them after they happened. But it's hard to be sure."

Karl added, "So what he's saying is, when you jump back and then come tell us what you did, forgive us if we don't believe you."

From that day on, training took on a new flavor. I focused on getting ready to jump back in time. In the mornings I kept up my conditioning, but we also worked on cold water training. A few days into it, they showed me why. Morris led me downstairs into a big walk-in freezer, like in a meat-packing plant. This room, similar to the one upstairs, had one wall of windows that looked in on a tunnel. But this one looked like it had been built without any kind of budget constraints. It was at least twice as big as the one I had seen. And instead of gray foil, the sides were white and smooth, like plastic, or even ceramic. The hundreds of cables running into it were all neatly bundled and zip-tied together.

On tables around the room were several gray boxes about the size of coffins. They looked like they were made out of wet plastic.

"This is what we launch into the Big Buddy. It's ice," explained Morris. "It's one thing we can build that will provide some shielding from the radiation and also leave no trace once you arrive. And best of all, it floats."

"Why is that the best thing?" I asked.

"Well, since we can only approximate the location you'll end up, the safest bet is to aim about ten feet above a body of water. Gives us plenty of room for error."

I studied the box. The top half was riddled with fist-sized

cutouts, almost like a basket. Air holes, I supposed. But the surface was almost opaque. "Why is it so… dirty looking? So gray?"

"It looks cloudy because they mix a paper slush in the water to add strength and impact resistance. Developed it in World War II. It's called Pykrete. We mold that thing in halves, and then seal the traveler inside by fusing the edges together right before the launch."

I didn't love the sound of "seal the traveler inside," but I kept it to myself.

My afternoons were no longer my previous classes. I was given several people to study. I sat in the monitor-filled surveillance room and watched video for hours. I figured out that I wasn't watching real time. The videos were from several years ago, and I was getting just highlights: when the people met or talked to each other. There were three people I was watching, all males. Two looked Middle-Eastern and one looked white, as best I could tell. They mostly spoke a slangy mash-up of Farsi and English that was tough to follow at first. The scrolling translations were a life-saver. Nobody would tell me what I was supposed to look out for, just that I should watch them. So I did, from multiple camera angles, mostly poorly lit, like from hidden cameras. There were also some shots where I guess we'd hacked the webcams on their laptops. This was a little unnerving, because it was like the guys were looking right at me. I saw hours of phone calls, TV watching, and gaming. When they texted, I got that on my translation screen also. Pretty slick. Within a few hours, I learned the names of the main players. Well, nicknames probably, but it was all they called each other.

Bowie seemed to be the leader, because the others usually deferred to him, and he never seemed to leave the apartment. He sat on the couch with his spotty beard and white t-shirt and sent the other two out to get things. Tuck, the white guy, was pudgy and perpetually sweating. He mostly came back with documents. Crow was taller and gangly, with long greasy hair. He usually showed up bearing shopping bags of food and clothes. Bowie would inspect them, and either approve or occasionally fly off the handle and scream at Crow for being an idiot. I learned a lot of new Farsi curse words. I wasn't sure what their roles were beyond that. But they spent a lot of time getting ready for the arrival of somebody named Ravit.

On my third day of watching, Morris came by to check on me. "Got a good feel for these guys?"

"I think so, yeah."

"Spoiler alert: you're going to be Ravit. So start growing a beard. We'll shave your head later."

"What?" I spluttered. "I'm... I don't know anything about being undercover. Or anything about Ravit."

Morris patted me on the back. "That's okay, they don't know anything about him either. Just that he learned to build bombs in Lebanon. Tomorrow you're going to start learning how to build bombs."

I guess my eyes bulged enough in reaction to that to get Morris's notice. He gave me his reassuring nod. "Relax. If they knew anything about explosives, they wouldn't be asking for Ravit. You won't have to know much to look like an expert."

I learned how to build a couple types of bombs. And I studied the videos with new focus. If Bowie and his buddies were planning to blow something up, they were very good at not mentioning anything specific on the tapes. I guess always assuming that you're under surveillance is Lesson Number One at terrorist trade school.

I asked Morris about it the next time we had lunch together. I felt a little dumb for not having figured out the answer myself already, but I wanted to know. "Hey, what is it these guys are going to blow up? Or already blew up, I guess."

Morris took an abnormally long time chewing his bite of sandwich before answering. "Believe me, we'll tell you when you need to know. Not right now. We found out the hard way that if we tell people too early they overthink it. You'll try to remember the event, you'll google it. You can't help yourself. But all that stuff just messes with your head and gets in the way. Especially if the media version isn't quite how it really went down. Just know that these guys aren't amateurs, they're Amrika Intifadah. I'll tell you the rest before the jump. And, that, by the way, is this Tuesday."

To my credit, I did not spit my food out in dramatic fashion. "Wow. Okay. What do I need to do to get ready?"

"Nothing special, you're already doing everything you need to do physically and mentally. Grow the beard. We'll give you the official prep list today, but it's nothing crazy. It's best if you fast for about twelve hours before, so you have less to puke. We'll have you sleep here on Monday night so you don't get stuck in traffic or anything."

Or get cold feet and run, I thought.

He smiled, which somehow emphasized his lack of chin. "And you don't have to worry about stopping your mail or anything, because you'll be back before you left." He laughed at that.

On Friday and Saturday morning I did practice landings: they put me in a plastic box and dropped me in the pool so I could get used to getting out without panicking. In the afternoon we studied maps. I learned the lay of the crappy part of Detroit where Bowie stayed, and how to get around the area. Of course Ravit wouldn't be expected to know any of this, so anything I learned should give me an edge.

Sunday I had the day off, but I was too keyed up to relax. You know me: right before a big work thing, I can't think about anything else. I tried to watch a movie, but I couldn't pay attention enough to follow the plot. Any time the actors talked, I imagined myself trying to convince strangers that I was a Lebanese terrorist.

On Monday morning, they wouldn't let me do anything strenuous. Couldn't have me getting hurt this close to the trip. I spent all morning watching tapes of the targets. I focused on what they talked about, what they laughed at, what made them nervous. I repeated what they said out loud, trying to match the rhythm of their speech. Morris walked in while I was talking to myself. I heard him laugh and looked back to see him smiling at me. "That's good, what you're doing. Prep always helps. But remember, these guys don't know Ravit and he doesn't know them. Anything you aren't prepared for will just seem authentic." He laid a folder down on the table in between us. "So here's the mission: we have high confidence that these are the guys that take down the Washington Monument." He pointed to a photo, that iconic one showing the remains of the obelisk, the two big halves lying askew across the grassy expanse of the Washington Mall, the White House in the background, the entire area cordoned off and surrounded by uniformed officers.

"Then why...?" I started, and then hesitated, not wanting to sound like I was trying to get out of the mission, but plunged on anyway: "Why don't the cops arrest them now if we know who did it? Or arrest them before they do it?"

"Valid question. You're always thinking, aren't you?" Morris nodded. "The problem is, we never have quite enough on surveillance to get a conviction. Never mind that we didn't exactly get a warrant for those surveillance cameras. But most importantly, right before the attack, they vanish with no warning. We never see them again." He made a sour face and shook his head at this. "So, what we need you to do is infiltrate their little club, confirm their target, and stop them. Irrevocably."

He paused and looked at me. I knew what he meant by "irrevocably." thinking back to my job interview with the simunition rounds. I realized he didn't want to say the words "kill them" out loud. I wasn't sure if he expected a response, so I nodded. He went on.

"And since they're organized in cells, you need to get these guys all at one place and one time. This may be the biggest challenge. Do whatever it takes to get them all at once. If any one of them gets away, they'll reorganize and reform. We gotta tear out the whole cell by the roots."

The thought of confronting them all at once was not comforting. It felt like a lot of things could go wrong. "What if the real Ravit shows up?"

Morris snorted, "Don't worry about that. We're dealing with him separately." He pushed back from the desk and leaned back. "Anything else? Everything clear?"

"Yeah, I guess so. You know, it's just I've never done anything like this before."

"Well, you're in pretty good company. Pretty much nobody has ever done anything like this before. Look at it this way: you're twice as prepared as anybody we've ever sent back."

Somehow that wasn't reassuring. "And how many people have we sent?"

"Well, it depends on how you keep score, but less than ten. As of now anyway."

Tuesday morning came, unstoppable like an approaching storm. I hadn't gotten much sleep on the cot in the locker room. The huge old empty building was full of weird noises at night, sudden creaking over constant mechanical humming. But despite that, I walked into the project hyper-alert. They shaved my head and I changed into my Ravit clothes, everything period-correct from two and a half years ago. I had a wallet with a Ravit ID. It said I was from Seattle.

No fancy weapons, in case I got stopped by a cop or something. I'd have to get whatever I needed when I arrived. Plus, we didn't want to ship any extra weight. But you know what's lightweight and transfers back just fine? Cash. I had bundles of old bills in plastic bags banded around my ankles and torso. Plenty enough for guns. Enough that if it all worked out, I should be able to lay low in someplace where I wouldn't run into myself until I lived back to the present. It wouldn't hurt that I knew who won the last couple of Superbowls too.

At 10:00 am, I went downstairs to the Big Buddy. Bill and Karl helped me lie down in my ice coffin. They'd scanned me yesterday, so it fit me tightly. The assembly table was on a scale so they would know the precise weight. I heard the telltale buzz of drones, then Dr. Verhagen stepped quickly into the room. He extended a hand to me and I awkwardly tried to sit up on the slippery ice to shake it.

"Good luck, Allen," he said in his detached voice. "This mission is of critical importance to our nation. I have no doubt that you are the right man for it."

I smiled and mumbled something about how I wouldn't let him down, and then he was gone. An overhead gantry crane set the upper half of the box on top of me. I watched through the air holes as Bill and Karl walked around me with compressed gas, freezing the two halves together. Then they slid the whole deal toward the launch chute. The big underground tunnel was already humming. Morris had told me that every time we ran this system, it pulled so much power from the local grid that even with all our internal capacity, our quadrant of Chicago would experience a brownout for a few minutes.

Morris leaned over a cutout in the ice above my face and said, "Break a leg, Ravit. Live your way back and come see me tomorrow." Then he stepped back and the techs closed the door of the chute.

My thoughts closed in on me like the darkness. What the hell was I doing? It all seemed so ordinary when Bill and Karl talked about it: business as usual. But now the enormity of how not normal this was hit me. How did I know this thing even worked? Because a few guys who I'd just met told me it did? How dangerous was this, really? I hadn't asked enough questions when I had the chance. I tried to breathe slowly and deeply like they'd taught me, but it didn't seem to help.

And then I moved, shot forward with brutal acceleration like that electromagnetic rollercoaster at Cedar Point. Fast and dark, the sound of the ice sliding in the metal of the tube. Then all the sound stopped, replaced by the stomach churning feeling of falling. I tried not to puke. Then I puked. I hadn't eaten, so it was just bile that came up, all over my face and shirt. Then bright light. Very bright compared to the chute. Sudden impact, a loud splash, and the frigid water rushed through the air holes onto my face and hands. I was thrown around as my big ice cube bobbed to the surface and rocked back and forth.

I pressed my hands against the ice like they'd taught me. Nothing, no movement. They had told me to be patient. The ice would melt and weaken enough for me to get out, like a chick emerging from an egg. But as the ice melted, wouldn't I ride lower in the water? What if I sank before I could break out? What if I was too heavy? We'd never practiced with the real reinforced ice in the freezing water of Lake Erie. What if they'd screwed up the calculations? I could drown, back here in the past, where nobody would be looking for me, where my only help was over two years away. The smell of vomit was all around me in this confining box. I thrashed and twisted, but there wasn't enough room to turn anywhere. The movement made the frigid water slosh around me. It started to cover my nose.

I breathed in for a count of three. It wasn't easy. I slowed down. Getting myself to breathe out was harder with the water creeping up higher. I calmed. Waited. I heard the ice groan, then crack somewhere under my lower back. I slowly jackknifed forward, and the ice under my butt broke. I pushed more and was able to wriggle out. The cool water felt like freedom.

I treaded water and looked around. I was alone out here. The gray morning sky met the darker gray water all the way around me, except for a dark green line of distant trees to my left. No signs of any buildings or boats. I swam for the shore, using the slow, energy-conserving strokes we'd practiced. I got stuck in stinking, sucking mud in the shallows, but finally trudged through scrubby grass onto a gravel road. A small sign greeted me that read "Vermet Unit PUBLIC HUNTING AREA."

It looked like they'd hit the region we were aiming for. I had just survived being launched several thousand miles in space, and hopefully a couple of years in time.

I picked a direction on the road that looked like it might lead to civilization and started walking. I was tired and increasingly cold. Maybe money could buy happiness, but it sucked for keeping you warm.

* * *

The trip from Lake Erie into Detroit was an ordeal. Nobody picks up a wet hitchhiker. Not a male one anyway. But after a few hours walking, I caught a ride with a hunter who bought my story about falling out of a boat. I even managed to resist asking him the date. A page of a recent-looking newspaper on the floor of the truck advertised a "2023 EASTER SALE-A-BRATION!" Looked like Bill and Karl had hit the date target too. I had travelled back in time. It was oddly anticlimactic. I was in the past, but a past I'd already lived through. It felt less like the *Wizard of Oz* and more like jet lag.

Once I made it into Detroit, I got a cheap and malodorous motel room four blocks from Bowie's apartment, from a guy who evidently was not alarmed at my wetness. This would give me a safe house and staging area if I needed it. I bought food and dry clothes at an imitation Wal-Mart, and then walked to a local pawn shop for weapons. There wasn't a lot available. Andre had primed me for this: when you're buying a used gun that your life might depend on, get the simplest thing you can. I settled on two Smith and Wesson .38 revolvers. In a rundown pawnshop, it cost surprisingly little to skip the three-day waiting period for gun purchases. I stuffed the bulk of my remaining cash above a ceiling tile in the motel room, then put the guns in plastic bags in the toilet tank. No point making housekeeping suspicious.

Satisfied with my back-up preparations, I caught a cab to Michigan Station and called the phone number I'd been given for Bowie. Whoever answered didn't say anything, so I started, "I'm here now. I could use a ride."

Bowie's voice, familiar from the tapes, finally responded: "That's good. We'll be there in fifteen minutes. Meet us out front. Gold Honda Accord."

"I'll be waiting."

Twenty minutes later, an Accord stopped at the curb. I walked over, smiling like I was greeting old friends. I recognized the driver as Crow, a baseball hat failing to hide his stringy hair. He rolled down the window and said, "What's your name?"

I didn't know if there was some kind of password, so I gave them the only answer I could. "Ravit."

He nodded and popped the door locks. I climbed into the back seat, next to Bowie. The color on the surveillance tapes hadn't been good, so I was unprepared for his dyed blond hair, but it finally clicked. Spiky blond hair, like David Bowie. He eyed me up and down, then said, "Good trip?"

I concentrated on getting the cadence right, without sounding like I was trying. "Bloody awful trip. And it's freezing here. But I expected that." They probably had no idea where Ravit was supposed to have come from. Bowie just nodded.

As we cleared the train station area, I got to take in the sad state of Detroit. The rumors of its resurgence have been exaggerated. There were a few businesses, but nothing with a name you'd recognize. And still plenty of abandoned shells. As I watched them roll by, Bowie said, "Pull in here." We turned into a burned-out husk of a building that must've been a fast food place, and stopped. This wasn't the apartment. When I turned to Bowie, he had a gray Glock pointed at me. "What's the recognition code?"

I had nothing. Pointed at me, the end of the barrel looked impossibly large. We were packed so tight in the back of the little car there was no room for any of the fancy disarming moves Andre had practiced with me. I was facing death for the first time in my life. My breath was short; this was not how I wanted to die. I thought of you lying in the hospital and wondered if anyone ever died the way they wanted to. But I had no idea what answer they were looking for. So I told them that.

"I don't know any recognition code." Bowie didn't fire, so I pressed on, trying to sound unconcerned. "I don't have time to read every stupid message they send. I was told to come here and build you a bomb. Do you want me to build you a bomb or not?"

Bowie considered this for an excruciating eternity that was probably ten seconds. Then he put the gun away and nodded to Crow, who backed us out. He drove us to the ancient apartment building I knew from the surveillance and dropped us at the curb.

Bowie said, "Tomorrow," to him, and Crow drove off.

I followed Bowie into the building. I knew the apartment was on the third floor. We headed up the fire stairs that stank of piss. As soon as we climbed past the landing for the second floor, the door banged open and Tuck rushed out carrying a duffle bag in one hand and an automatic pistol in the other. He was sweating even more than I was used to.

"Stop!" he hissed, and held a finger to his lips. Bowie's face was curious but calm, and he didn't say a thing. Tuck went on in a loud whisper, "I found a bug in the apartment. I don't know how long it's been there. We can't go back in there." Then, still looking at Bowie, he pointed with the gun towards me. "I bet it's this guy. I find a bug the same day he shows up? That can't be a coincidence. I bet he's a Fed."

Bowie looked at me expectantly. I resisted the impulse to put my hands up. Tuck was at best a step and a half away from me, and holding the gun too loosely. I could get there and take it before he could get a shot off. But then what? I might not get Bowie in time, and I had no way to get Crow. Now wasn't the time, so I tried to reason with him. "Look, I just came to build the bombs. If I was a cop, what would be the point of bugging your place too? That doesn't make any sense."

Tuck did not look at all convinced by my logic. But Bowie seemed satisfied. He motioned for Tuck to lower the gun, and Tuck reluctantly obeyed, still watching me.

Tuck whispered, "Where do we go now?"

Bowie shrugged. "Let me think."

Figuring I had nothing to lose, I volunteered, "I have a motel room near here." They both looked at me like I was changing colors.

"And why do you have a motel room?" asked Bowie.

"Because I didn't know if I could trust you fuckers."

* * *

We walked to my motel after I assured them I'd registered

under a fake name. Tuck kept jerking his head around, sure cops were going to spring from every alley. On the way, Bowie looked down at Tuck's duffle bag. "How much did you get out of the apartment?"

"Everything incriminating," Tuck panted. "I got the maps, the uniforms. All I left was groceries."

We climbed the iron stairs to room 217, where Bowie flopped onto the bed, while Tuck meticulously looked behind all the lamps and generic framed pictures, presumably searching for bugs. He didn't manage to find my money or my guns. I guess he'd never seen *The Godfather*.

I started to sit, but Bowie said, "Don't get comfortable. We've got a meeting to buy explosives and detonators in two hours" — slowly, like he was choosing each word carefully. "Our faces are probably known to the Feds now. I need you to go make the pick-up."

So I could get arrested alone, I thought. And what happens then? Would Project Never get me out of trouble? The project didn't even exist yet. The thought crossed my mind to shoot these two now and look for Crow later. But I might never find him.

"Fine. Just tell me how I'm getting there," I said, hoping to sound like this was no big deal to me. "And how much I'm getting."

"Crow rented a minivan this morning. It's parked behind the apartment. You'll be getting two-hundred and eighty pounds of Semtex, and five detonators," answered Bowie, without moving from the bed.

I still hadn't confirmed what their target was, so I pushed a little: "Are you sure we'll have enough?"

Bowie cocked his head curiously at me. "We're buying all he's got. It'll be enough."

So much for that. Bowie handed me keys while Tuck pulled a bunch of stuff out of his duffle bag. He eventually came up with a roll of hundred-dollar bills that he gave to me. As he stuffed papers and clothes back into the bag, I saw a beige shirt with a brown patch on the sleeve: "Parks Department, Washington D.C."

Bingo. Washington Monument.

The meet was about an hour and a half away, at a busy gas station off Highway 75. When I got there, the seller had his panel van parked around to the side, next to an overfull dumpster. I circled the building, seeing lots of work trucks, but nothing that looked like cops, so I parked next to him and got out.

With sunglasses and a blue beanie hat, the seller didn't look at all out of place with the rest of the clientele, who seemed to be mostly construction workers getting off work and buying tall beers and individual cigars. Chances are he was just a demolition worker who needed some extra money. I was the one who felt conspicuous, like everyone was checking me out. I thought about how you always got nervous in sketchy places like this, and I wondered how I'd ended up in one, buying explosives. When, exactly, did I sign up for this?

He opened the back door of the van and pulled out a little eight-ounce block of Semtex, still in the original plastic. It looked like pale-yellow modeling clay, just like it was supposed to. I didn't know any other way to tell if it was real other than smell it, so I cut into the plastic with my pocket knife. It smelled like spicy paint, just like I remembered from training. The whole van was filled with big, unmarked cardboard boxes.

"Two hundred eighty pounds. You wanna look in the boxes?"

I really didn't. I didn't care if he was ripping me off, since I didn't actually want Bowie and his lackeys to be able to blow anything up. But I didn't want to alarm this guy, so I pointed at a box at random. "Yeah, show me that one." The box was fine, and the detonators were industrial demolition units just like I expected.

Two hundred and eighty pounds of Semtex. Seeing that much of it really brought home the stakes. There was a lot of death in these boxes. In my old timeline, I'm fairly sure nobody died when they took the Washington Monument down. But this was a whole new event. If I screwed things up, or spooked the boys into changing plans, they could take out a couple of city blocks, anywhere.

I gave Beanie-Hat the money. It took us almost ten minutes to move the boxes from his van to mine. The level of hyper-alert paranoia I experienced while transferring black market explosives under the bright streetlights was completely new to me. None of the locals paid us any obvious attention, but it did give me an idea that might solve my biggest problem: getting everyone together in one place.

On the drive back, I called Bowie on the disposable phone he'd given me. I forced calm in my voice: "Everything went fine. I'm headed back. We're going to want all the hands we can get to unload this quick. Don't want to spend any more time attracting attention on the sidewalk than we have to."

"Yeah, good thinking. I'll have the guys ready when you get here."

I obeyed every traffic law and kept it five miles an hour under the speed limit, basically driving like your step-dad, and you know how hard that is for me. But nobody stopped me. It was nine o'clock when I got back.

The gold Accord was parked down the block. Crow climbed out to meet me. We each grabbed a box from the van and toted it to the motel room, where Bowie and Tuck were leaned over a newspaper, scanning the classified ads. There they were: all three of them in the same room. I might not get this chance again. I had to act now.

I dropped my box on the bed and announced, "If I don't piss, I'm going to die," as I headed to the bathroom. Really? Did I have to say *die*?

I really did have to piss, but as I flushed I lifted the cover off the toilet tank. Still there. I put the revolver with the 4" barrel in my waistband. The little snubnose had come with an ankle holster and I strapped that to my left calf — redundancies and backup plans, just like Morris would say. My heart was beating hard and too fast. I took some deep breaths before I realized I'd probably been in the bathroom a suspiciously long time. I walked out, trying out a casual saunter.

Crow was coming in the door carrying a box, followed by Bowie. I walked past them toward the door, and stopped with my back to them. I knew where everyone was, knew all the angles. But I couldn't make my hand draw the gun. This wasn't training anymore, these were real bullets. My heart was pounding so hard I could hear the throb in my ears.

Bowie said, "Did you bring me any change, Ravit?" That broke my paralysis. I was tempted to give some sarcastic answer, but the last thing I needed was to draw attention to myself. I got the gun barrel clear of my pants as I turned back to face him.

His eyes opened wide as I quickly closed the distance, shoved the barrel into his chest, and pulled the trigger. The gun made a sound like a loud sneeze. Bowie crumpled. Crow spun toward me, dropping his box and reaching toward his belt. With two fast steps, I got my left ankle behind his as he tried to retreat. I swept out with my arm, pushing him back over my leg, and followed him down. My gun was pressing his solar plexus when I fired, again using his body to muffle the report.

I turned toward the door to see Tuck standing there. He yelled, "I knew it!" before he backed out the door. I was up and after him, having to hurdle the box he'd dropped. I figured he'd be running away, but I exited the door low, just in case. I turned to see Tuck, three feet from the door frame, bringing his big automatic pistol to bear on me. It seemed these guys had some kind of combat training after all.

Not wanting to make the noise of shooting in the open, I sprang forward and pushed his elbow so his arm continued its swing, past me and across his body. I tried the ankle lock trick again, but Tuck was lunging toward me. He was too heavy for me to stop him, and he fell on top of me. He brought his knee up and pinned my arm to the concrete walkway. He put some weight behind it and I felt my right wrist pop. The rest of him crushed down on my chest as he tried to push himself up. I couldn't take a good breath; ribs were cracking as I drew from my ankle holster with my left hand. I got the small revolver under his armpit and fired twice before he could get his automatic aimed at me. He fell back and didn't move.

I pushed him off me and sat up to scan the area. The gun hadn't made much noise, but we'd been wrestling outside, and that was likely to attract the attention of anyone nearby. I needed to get us inside quickly. I didn't want some local street entrepreneur to nose around and end up with a bunch of Semtex. Thinking back, Morris had told me to "call it in," but I wasn't exactly sure what that meant.

I pulled Tuck inside the room, my right wrist grinding in objection, and wiped both of my guns off with a washcloth from the bathroom. I didn't have time to stage much of a crime scene, but I wanted to give a lazy cop something plausible to discover. I put my primary gun in Tuck's hand, and my backup gun in Crow's hand. Good enough.

I picked up the ancient landline phone in the room and called 911.

"Yes, I'm at the Starlite Motel on Dragoon. There are some

Middle-Eastern looking guys next door, and I think I heard gunshots. Yes, they're in room 217." I hung up.

My heart was still racing, both from exertion and adrenaline. I had just killed three people. Three bad people. I expected an overwhelming feeling of remorse or something. But it was more like relief. I was done. In fact, I didn't even have to be Ravit anymore. I was just Allen D'auria again.

So what did Allen D'auria do on this day in history in 2023? I glanced down at the newspaper on the table. Well, tomorrow was a Thursday, so he goes to work. The date hit me as I tried to sit down on the bed. Only about half my ass made it and I fell on the floor. Tomorrow, at work, Allen would get a phone call. It would be the cops calling, telling him that you'd been hit by a car.

* * *

There was really no chance of me not going to the site. There I was, on the day before you died, six hundred miles away. I would have run there if I had to. But I didn't; I drove the rented van, not even taking the time to finish unloading it.

I thought back to the day you died, trying to remember everything I could about the accident. The police report just listed the intersection of 1st Avenue and St. Mark's, but that was really quite a bit of area. My memory of that whole period was so jumbled, I couldn't come up with the exact time it happened. So I got there early, about 9:15 the next morning, and I waited and I watched.

I bought a coffee and leaned against a construction scaffold on 1st Avenue, trying to stay out of the intermittent spring drizzle. I scanned all sides of the intersection constantly, grumbling and darting aside whenever an umbrella or vehicle blocked my view. I'm sure I looked like some kind of weirdo; I'm a little surprised the cops never hassled me.

A few minutes before eleven, I saw you. It was the first

time I'd seen you in almost three years. You walked down St. Marks and turned onto 1st, going away from me, and it was like those years never happened. You were wearing black leggings and that print top with the giant red flowers you loved. Your hair kept getting blown into your face, and you brushed it back. I couldn't breathe.

I stood up to go to you, to meet you, stop you. I ran across 1st Street, pushing through the crowd, trying to keep you in sight. I just had to get across St. Marks.

Someone grabbed me from behind. An arm snaked under my shoulder and wrapped around the back of my neck in a half nelson. I spun right, trying to twist free like I was taught, but they had planned for that, and used my own force to pull me off the sidewalk and into the doorway of a bar.

"Redundancies and back-ups, Allen," said a voice I knew. Morris's voice, the Boston accent strong. "Did you think you were the only operative sent back heah?" He didn't wait for an answer. "Verhagen expected you to try this. He sent me to keep you on task." I tried to turn around but he had me pressed against the wall, my arm twisted behind me. "You're here to stop a bombing."

"But she's going to die! All I have to do is warn her!" I struggled and he twisted my arm tighter.

"You don't get it," Morris hissed into my ear. "We recruited you because you were a loner with no family. If you save your wife, then you never join the project, and the bombers take out the Washington Monument. We can't let you save her."

"Who cares about the goddamn monument? They don't even kill anybody!" My head was pushed against a dusty wall.

"No," Morris answered. "But having the Washington Monument destroyed on his watch, and never catching the bombers, costs President Everett the election. Think of it, that giant phallus getting knocked down two blocks from the White House... talk about looking impotent. The next president misuses the project, starts aborting his opponents. We warned ourselves from the future: we need to stop the bombing."

I couldn't listen to him talking about finishing the mission. All I could see was you in the red print top brushing your hair back. That image was blotted out by one of your bloated body, full of tubes, in the hospital.

Then Morris's words sank in.

Morris didn't know I'd already finished the mission. I'd stopped the bombing. Nobody knew; it had all happened off camera. Morris wouldn't risk hurting me, because he thought he still needed me.

I let my legs go slack, holding my breath against the coming pain. My arm twisted and my shoulder started to dislocate. Morris let his hold slip so he wouldn't break my arm. It gave me enough room to turn on the way down and kick his left leg out from under him. When he fell toward me, my left arm came around like Andre had trained me, and I struck Morris in the throat, letting out all my breath and pain and fear. It knocked his head back against the floor and he went limp, blood matting his hair. Unconscious or dead, it didn't matter to me then.

I jumped up and ran back out to the sidewalk. I yelled your name, spinning frantically to find you. You were on my side of the street now, fifty feet away. You stopped and turned, looking at me without recognition. I ran toward you, yelling. With my beard and shaved head, you had no idea who I was.

The brown car jumped the curb and hit you from behind. Your knees crumpled sideways and your head bounced off the windshield with a wet thunk, like a melon hitting concrete. My feet dragged to a walk. You were carried on the hood, your leg dragging on the ground, until the Camry swerved back onto the street, clipping another pedestrian in the process. People were screaming, jumping out of the way. You rolled off the hood of the car and onto the sidewalk, and I couldn't see you anymore. I bent low and watched the car as it passed me, gaining speed. The driver was unmistakable. No chin at all, and with more hair than I'd ever seen on him. Then Morris was gone, speeding down the startlingly traffic-free street. That was probably the car he'd pick me up in two years from now.

I ran to you, pushing people out of the way. The police held me back. As many times as I'd pictured this in my head, the reality was worse. Here, with crowds of people turning away and hiding their faces in horror, was your bent, bleeding body in a heap. I turned away too, sobbing. I found myself back at the doorway of the bar where I'd left Morris. But Morris was gone, just like I knew he would be.

The city was gray and silent for me as I walked back to the van.

* * *

I guess I need to wrap this letter up, because I'm headed to see Professor Verhagen give a lecture at NYU in a couple hours. There won't be any fancy bomb sniffing security around him yet, not in 2023. They won't stop me, no matter how much Semtex I'm carrying. And I don't think the project will have a back-up plan for this, because they'll never exist. Anymore. Anywhen. If it works out, you'll see it in the papers. The media will probably blame it on Amrika Intifada.

I know I haven't been available enough. Or paid enough attention to you. And I've been kind of an asshole. But know that if you're reading this, it's because I changed history for you. So maybe, when you see me, you can give me another chance. I'll do better this time.

* * * * *

I figure that if you fancy yourself a science-fiction writer, you probably need to take a stab at time travel eventually. I found myself thinking: if you instantly transported in time, how does a time machine know WHERE to send you, since the earth is in motion? This story came out of those musings, and it involved drawing a bunch of complicated looping timeline diagrams.

ANNIHILATOR

"HELL BROKE LOOSE, Could Not More Appall the Good People of the Capital City Than the Dark and Damnable Deeds Done in the Blackness of Night By Fiends"

Headline of the Fort Worth Gazette, December 26, 1885

"In 1885, Austin, Texas, was terrorized by a serial killer known as the 'Servant Girl Annihilator.'… he claimed eight victims, mostly black servant girls, all attacked in the dark of night… The city had no outdoor lighting until 1894, when it decided to buy more moonlight in the form of towers. They were 15 stories tall, each crowned with a circle of six lights soaring way up above the city."

Slate.com, January 28, 2015

Tuesday, January 19, 1886 - Austin, Texas

The girl moaned as he dragged her into the yard. She was beginning to wakeThe girl moaned as he dragged her into the yard. She was beginning to wake up, which was alright. It worked better if she was awake for this part. He straddled her and sat on her thin chest to keep her from moving. His weight forced air from her lungs, blowing out as vapor in the cold air. He pinned her skinny arms under his knees, put the bloody axe on the ground, then reached into the satchel that held his implements. The wooden spike he withdrew, no larger than a pencil, glistened in the moonlight, the pale wood stained a shiny black with years of dried blood. At the small end of the spike, lashed in place like an arrowhead, was the sharp bone from the second toe on his right foot. He pressed the dark skin of the girl's face to the frigid earth. The sudden cold must've shocked her awake, because she gasped. He began singing a low, warbling summoning song while he placed the bone tip of the spike in her left ear, then raised his right hand, ready to strike it and drive the bone home as soon as he felt the response to the song: the pressure of ancient attention.

Annihilator. People had started calling him the Servant Girl Annihilator. The newspapers hadn't picked that name up yet, but he'd heard it said in two different taverns in town. They couldn't be more wrong. The last thing he wanted to do was annihilate the girls. To annihilate them would be to wipe them out, erase them from existence. He needed to do the opposite: to make them into luminous beacons, like bonfires, that would call down the attention of his benefactors. There was power in naming something, but it had to be the right name. Servant Girl Annihilator wasn't close enough to the truth to mean anything to him.

People also called him a monster. They didn't know what that word meant either. He was just a man, a man who was required to do some terrible things. He knew what monsters were. He had spoken to them. And if he didn't hear from them again soon, he would die.

"There!" A woman's shout came from the back of the house. He turned to see the light of a lantern swinging wildly, moving closer to him. "Somebody's out there by the swing! He's got Josephine!"

Damn it! There wouldn't be time to finish the summoning ceremony itself, much less any time to enjoy the girl. This was turning out just like December. He pushed off of the girl and struggled to his feet. Placing the spike in his pouch, he pulled out a handful of pungent black powder that he flung behind him as he fled. The powder would blind and confuse any pursuers long enough to let him outdistance them, even with his hobbling gait.

He made it down the street and onto his horse before anyone had gotten out of the yard. The black horse ran hard, but its hooves made no noise on the hard-packed dirt of Guadalupe Street.

He was safely away, but the night had been a failure. His rites were becoming less effective. Last spring, when he'd offered up the first several girls, his intrusions had been undetectable, at least long enough to do what was needed. But lately people in the houses had been discovering him too soon. It was like the spirits weren't listening to his communications any longer. Maybe they weren't listening to anybody anymore. He'd have to find a new way to get their attention; his life depended on it.

* * *

Sunday, May 5, 1895 - Austin, Texas

Nicholas Raeburn left his office at the university ten minutes after noon, walking briskly. The day was already warm, giving the people of Austin a glimpse of the baking summer that was just around the corner. He'd wanted to pick up flowers on the way home for lunch, but he was already late. Would the added delay of stopping for flowers make her angrier or happier? It was hard to tell anymore.

Dodging a horse, he turned the corner to Guadalupe Street, sidestepping idle children, hurrying past the bent old man on the bench smoking an awful-smelling pipe. As Nicolas opened the stout wooden gate in front of the imposing three-story Victorian house, Fausto leaped to his feet and came bounding forward, snarling, teeth bared. When he got close enough to recognize Nicholas, he became his usual tail-wagging ball of bumbling energy.

Nicholas scratched Fausto behind the ears while he pried off his dusty boots on the front porch. Josephine stuck her head around the corner of the porch. "You might want to hurry. They waited on you."

Nicholas started to reply, but she was gone before he could. He followed her across the porch to the side of the house and saw her in the large side yard, hanging laundry on the line. He wanted to go to her, talk to her. But she was right, his mother was waiting.

He found his mother seated at the lunch table, her white hair collected in a severe bun, her starched blue dress defying the heat. She was flanked by two of Nicholas's young nephews and, to his surprise, his older cousin, Brandon. Smiling, Nick seated himself. His mother rang the bell for service without saying a word.

"I didn't expect you today," Nick said to Brandon. "When did you get here?"

"Came in just this morning," Brandon answered. "We needed a few things in town. Coffee and sugar…" He poked at his salad. "And I came to ask you a favor…" His sheepish smile crinkled the lines in his tanned face. "I could use your help with the herd sometime in the next couple of days. We need to brand and castrate the—" Nick's mother snorted in distaste at this. "I'm sorry, Aunt Marie." Then to Nick: "But it's more calves than we can handle in a day. I know it's not your favorite place," he said, glancing quickly at the scar down the left side of Nick's neck. "I wouldn't ask if it wasn't pressing."

Nick touched the scar absently and mustered some cheer. "Happy to help, Brandon. It'll be good to get outside for a while. I've just got an introductory physics class to teach tomorrow. We could leave right after that."

"Now, don't you go making extended plans," said Nick's mother. "Nicholas, you're to be here Wednesday night for the moontower debut." She held up an ornate cream-colored envelope and withdrew a card that had an embossed image of a full moon on the front. "We contributed good money to get the towers moved here from Detroit, and we will certainly be seen at their first lighting. Donating money and not getting recognized for it is worse than not giving the money in the first place." Glancing at the invitation, she continued: "The dedication is scheduled for 8:00 pm, but we will arrive a good bit earlier."

Nicholas managed a weak smile that didn't mask his discomfort, but Brandon chimed in: "You don't have to worry. We'll get it done tomorrow, and I'll have him back here Tuesday morning."

"You see that you do," said Marie, her glower showing that she was unconvinced. "I do not intend to go alone."

"Now that you mention it," said Nick, "I was thinking we could give the servants the night off. Let them go down for the debut, too. It's supposed to be quite a spectacle."

Mrs. Raeburn pursed her lips in disapproval. "Nicholas, I'm not blind you know," she said. "I know you like to have

Josephine close to you. And maybe at the ranch house that's acceptable. But it's really not done here in town." Her voice softened: "But if it will get you to go, we can think about it." Just then the youngest nephew dropped a fork. It rang on the floor and Fausto leapt up, barking ferociously. Nick put his hand on the dog's head to calm him, happy for any distraction from this line of conversation. "And if the moontowers really brighten the night," his mother continued, "and discourage criminals the way the mayor claims, maybe we could have a smaller, more attractive fence to replace these... prison walls we have now. And Fausto could move out to the ranch, where his protectionism would be more appreciated."

Nick took a deep breath. "Maybe we can think about that, too."

* * *

From his vantage point on the bench across the street, he could observe the Raeburn house. The girl hanging laundry might be the one he sought. His eyes weren't keen enough to be sure at this distance, and binoculars would draw unwanted attention.

His special mix of pipe tobacco, cloves, and coriander produced a telling smoke when he exhaled. The fumes had made him tear up and choke that first time he'd tested it. Now, after many decades of use, he'd come to crave the sickly-sweet smell. As he blew the smoke out, he pulled small bits of hair from his pocket and threw them into the air. The hair drifted down and to his right, carried by the almost unnoticeable breeze in the stifling heat that passed for spring in Texas. He watched and smiled in satisfaction as the smoke curled up and to the left, against the air current. Toward the girl. The smoke didn't lie.

He watched her affix the wet clothes to the line, which was tied to the tall cedar fence that enclosed the yard. The large dog lay close to her, a dozing pile of malicious muscle. The dog would be no concern when the time came, but the fence might pose problems. And the time must come soon. It had been too long, nine long years — they weighed on him, dragging his limbs toward the hungry earth.

She stooped to get more wet washing. Fine men's clothes. Dandy clothes. They whispered of money the same way the big house shouted it, yellow limestone and porticoes, ornamentation and immaculate grounds. She never left the property without one or more escorts, even for the smallest shopping errand. This he had noted. She bent again for the next fancy shirt, and he saw, peeking out from under the lifted hem of her gray cotton skirt, the long knife strapped to her ankle. Her right ankle. He would note that, too.

She had grown taller since they last saw each other. Nine years ago she had been a lanky and slight teenager, almost gaunt. Now she was a young woman, still fine of bone, and with the same mocha skin, but the years had brought with them full breasts and womanly hips. She would be harder to overpower now. But just as she had grown, so had his knowledge and abilities. The added years of her life should make the ceremony even more effective.

For now, he watched. Just an unassuming old man smoking a pipe. Sooner or later her protectors would grow lax. And he would be ready.

* * *

"Josie, have you seen my duster? I can't seem to find it." Nick pushed clothes back and forth in his closet, not finding anything suitable for the ride to the ranch. walked to the doorway and watched him search for a moment longer, a slight smirk on her face, "Did you look in the chair, right next to your bag? Under your hat, along with everything else you'll need, cowboy."

Nick turned to look at the chair and saw the long duck

cloth coat lying neatly exactly as she described it, right where she'd probably laid it out sometime this morning. He laughed. "I guess that settles it, I need you to come with me or I'll never be able to find anything."

"Don't tease me," she said, as she leaned over to make his bed. "You know your mother would never let me go. Besides, you and Brandon drink too much when you get together out there."

"Sometimes you like it when I drink too much," said Nicholas conspiratorially. He gave her a pat on the butt as he passed behind her to grab his gear.

Josephine jumped. "Dammit! You know I hate to be snuck up on!" Then she calmed herself and added in a whisper, "And if your mother saw you do that, she'd never let us be on the same floor without a chaperone. I think she's already got the cook telling her everything I do."

Nicholas laughed. "She probably should. You've been tempting me into misbehaving since we were five years old."

Her eyebrows shot up in bemused outrage. "I tempt *you*?" Her face grew serious, and Nick saw the guardedness return to her. For most of the last nine years, she had built a wall around herself. No little show of delight of anger escaped her unbidden. Each movement, each expression, was second-guessed before being allowed into the world. There was none of the easy laughter he'd grown up with. "You better be careful out there. Don't let Brandon talk you into doing anything dangerous. You ain't got to prove anything to him, just because you live in the big city now." Her eyes had a pleading look, almost desperation behind them. "You know how I hate it when you're gone."

Nick knew it was the wrong time to joke with her, and matched her serious tone as he reached into his jacket pocket and pulled out the small Colt revolver. "I want you to keep this in your bedside drawer while I'm gone," he said, and held out the blue steel gun.

Josephine pulled her hand back and shook her head. "I don't want that thing. I want you to have it out there. Between rattlesnakes and javelina, you're going to have use for it. What am I going to do if I find out you needed it but it was sitting here in my room?"

Nick hesitated, then placed it back in his pocket. "Alright." Smiling, he added, "I'll be extra careful, because I won't have you there to save me if I'm not. Wednesday will be here before you know it. I'm trying to talk Mother into letting the whole house off to go to the moontower debut that night." Nick watched her face but saw no reaction to that. "Do you want me to bring anything from the ranch house?"

"You just see that you bring your own self back from that ranch — with no extra holes in you this time." She placed a finger on the scar on his neck and Nick flinched, expecting it to hurt. After glancing furtively at the door, she leaned in and kissed him quickly on the lips. Before Nick could do anything to reciprocate, she was traipsing down the hallway with more lightness of spirit than he'd seen in her in years. He watched her swaying hips until she was out of sight.

* * *

When the old man had seen the Raeburn son leave that morning, trotting off with the other young man, he'd decided tonight would have to be the night. He couldn't wait much longer, and this would be his best chance.

He rushed back to his house to finish the preparatory ceremonies. First, he purified and treated the axe, rubbing wax into the runes etched into its face. It should make almost no sound tonight, no matter what it hit. He consecrated the bone-tipped spike at the same time, since the procedures were so similar, even though he didn't expect to need it for another day at least. Fortunately, he'd made up the confounding powder ahead of time. The only task left was to make himself unobservable to the dogs. He always saved this rite for last, since the effect wore off the fastest.

The sweet perfume of tropical plants filled the dim greenhouse at the back of his house. He inhaled deeply, knowing that verdant smell was about to be replaced by something less pleasant. Brushing overreaching leaves aside, he crossed to the tiny stone altar in the center of the room. His back protested as he bent low to light the candle that had long since melted to the top of the age-blackened dog skull. The gray wax began to drip, and he started singing a low warbling song he hadn't needed for almost ten years. He sprinkled the dried herbs into the candle flame to prime it. They sparkled as they ignited, and he leaned in to test their pungent smoke. Then he uncapped the vial of dog blood, and unsheathed the tiny lancet he wore on a leather lanyard around his neck. Quickly, he made a small, practiced cut on the side of his middle finger, next to dozens of tiny scars.

So many cuts along all his fingers, so much of the fluid of life spilled for the spirits. He wondered, as he often did, at the Oldest Ones' thirst for blood. What was it about blood that got their attention, more so than anything else? He let the dark red liquid drip from his finger onto a small copper dish, poured in the dog blood, and watched them swirl and mix as he held the dish over the flame. The mixture bubbled and the horrible smell was immediate and gut wrenching, easily overpowering the scents of the foreign flowers that crowded the room. All the while, he never stopped the low song, singing as loud as his rasping voice allowed. He dipped a finger into the hot liquid and used it to draw a line on his face from cheek to cheek, across the bridge of his nose. It was hot, and it stank. It stank like power. As the familiar pressure built in his ears he spread his arms and inhaled the stench along with the nighttime air.

He packed the black confounding powder in his satchel

with the bindings. At the last second, he decided to add the spike to his inventory. If the plan went awry and he couldn't abduct her, he might as well kill her tonight and hope for the best, hope the Oldest Ones would pay some notice. He doubted he'd live long enough to get a third chance at her if he failed this time.

When the blood had dried, he blew out the candle and went out the rear of the house, putting on his overcoat and slinging the satchel over his shoulder. When he reached the backyard stable, he rolled the axe in a blanket and tied it to the saddle. One last check of the horse's hooves for the sigils he had drawn on them. It was dark enough now to leave. The cloudy sky hid the moon as he rode into the woods behind the house.

The black horse cantered quickly and quietly through the empty streets, and finally turned up the hill to Guadalupe Street. The man dismounted and tied the horse to a fence slat thirty yards from the Raeburn house. He stayed close to the shadow of the fence, and crept toward the corner. There was no possibility of him climbing the fence in his present feeble condition. It stood at least six feet high, with each picket narrowed to a sharp point at the top. Instead, he dragged a hand across the wood until he came to the warped board he had noticed in his observations. He stuck the axe head behind the bowed surface and levered the handle outward. After a moment of laboring against the wood, he was able to pry the board out. With that picket gone, he wedged the board next to it free, giving himself enough space to slip inside.

As he stepped through the hole, the dog raised its head curiously, both ears up, and surveyed the yard. Its gaze swept right past the man, never registering a change. Then it yawned and returned its huge head to resting on the porch. The rite was working as intended, for now.

Her window was the last on the back left corner of the

house, fortunately on the ground level. He'd made it into second floor windows of other houses before, but not when he was feeling this… aged. The axe made only the smallest noise as it punched through the glass window, the quieting charm doing its work, and even the shards hitting the floor inside sounded like faraway tinkling. The sill inside had been stacked with bottles and jars, probably placed to raise a racket if anyone came in the window. Luckily, the spell on the axe extended to anything it hit. He carefully removed the two jars that hadn't fallen, placed them outside in the grass, then climbed awkwardly through the opening, pulling the heavy axe in behind him.

He gave his eyes time to grow accustomed to the darkness. Amid the gray shapes of plain wooden furniture, he found the girl's bed to his left. The slow rise and fall of her chest assured him that she was still asleep.

He pulled the packet of dark powder from his bag and withdrew a two-finger pinch. This he gently sprinkled above the sleeping girl's face, and waited for her to inhale its essence. Pulling a cloth from his satchel, he wrapped it around the axe head in preparation for the trickiest part: to hit her hard enough to knock her unconscious but not kill her.

When his eyes returned to hers, she was staring at him. She drew in a breath to scream, but he covered her mouth before the cry could escape. The confounding powder hadn't worked long on her at all. She struggled, shaking her head to get free of his hand, reaching for her right ankle. He cursed himself for not getting rid of the knife strapped there first, but he hadn't planned on her waking up. He couldn't risk releasing her mouth and letting her scream. He drew the axe back. Somehow she freed the knife and swung it. The blade caught his left forearm on an awkward upstroke. He felt it cut through jacket and shirt, but he couldn't let that stop him. He slammed the blunt end of the axe into the side of her head and her struggling ceased.

He gripped his left arm, trying to gauge how badly he was cut. It was a thin gash; blood slowly seeped out. Some had dripped on the wood floor, and he instantly wiped it up with his sleeve to ensure none would run between the boards and reach the ground below. There was nothing he could do about the tiny amount that had soaked into the wood. Hopefully it was too little to be used against him. He pulled strips of cotton cloth from the satchel. After binding the girl's wrists and gagging her, he still had enough left to bandage his own arm.

He stopped to listen for a long moment, hearing no sounds of anyone stirring in the house. He grabbed the girl under the armpits and wrenched her out of her bed, wincing at the loud thumps her feet made as they hit the floor. Dragging her to the broken window, his feet crunched on shards of glass. If she got cut, it was her own fault for her trick with the jars; it couldn't be helped. He'd have to check her later to make sure she didn't bleed to death.

Ten years ago, when he was stronger and she was smaller, carrying her out the window hadn't even been a concern. Now it took every ounce of his strength to heft her over the windowsill. She landed hard, head first, and he could hear her grunt as the wind was forced out of her. He climbed awkwardly out after her.

In his current decrepit state, he wasn't strong enough to carry her, so he dragged her across the yard. This was unfamiliar territory for him. In the past, when the Oldest Ones' attention had been easier to attract, he'd done the ceremony and finished the girls off right there in their yards and left them. Taking her with him was hard work and slow going.

He had been dragging her for several minutes and was still fifteen feet from the fence. He stopped to catch his breath.

This was taking much longer than he'd planned.

Just as he feared, the dog was starting to become aware of him. Its nose twitched, then its head popped up, gazing around. The man stood absolutely still. Apparently the dog still couldn't see him; it continued surveying the yard. The man started dragging the girl again. The dog turned toward the sound. The charm was wearing off, but there was nothing to be done about it now. The man redoubled his efforts; the fence was only eight feet away. The dog climbed down off the porch and walked slowly toward him, sniffing the ground. The man reached the fence and began climbing backwards through the gap, his hands laced together under the girl's breasts, pulling her with him.

Suddenly the dog barked and hurled himself at them. The man was still struggling to pull the girl over the lower fence stringer when the dog's teeth tore at his fingers, biting into them again and again. He yanked his hands back, and pulled the girl by the back of her nightdress. The dog clawed at the fence itself and barked. The noise was incredible and unceasing, splitting the silence like an alarm bell. A window lit up in the Raeburn house, then one in a neighboring home. He pulled out a fistful of the black powder and threw it at the dog. He didn't know if it worked on animals, but he could think of no other options. The beast snorted and sneezed, and then left the fence and began running around in circles. But still it barked. Unfortunately a confused dog was still a loud dog.

There was no way the man could drag the girl to the horse; it would take entirely too long. He made his decision and ran as best he could with his lopsided, limping gait to where it was tied. He freed the reins, climbed astride, and galloped to the girl, all concern for stealth abandoned. From the horse's back he could see another light now over the Raeburn fence, this one in the girl's window, and hear voices coming from inside. He dismounted, and with a hand on the horse's face, commanded it to sit all the way down on its haunches, like a sphinx. As he draped the girl over the horse's back, he heard a door of the house slam open, and shouts inside the fence. But they were too late, he was back on the horse and away. He spurred it to full gallop, one arm behind him to hold onto the girl. He hazarded a look back. Several people were running into the street. He saw the flash and heard the report of a shot, but he was already well beyond the reach of anyone but a sharpshooter.

He urged the horse on a twisting route through the unlit back streets of town. By the time they reached the obscured entrance into the woods that led to his house, the horse had resumed its nearly silent trot. He tried to get his own breathing under control. He began to relax. He had made this late-night escape so many times, the horse knew the way by itself. A long sigh exited his smirking mouth. It hadn't gone exactly smoothly, but now he had the girl all to himself... at long last.

* * *

Nick was up before sunrise on Tuesday, ready to get back to Austin. His muscles still ached from the work, much like his head ached from the whiskey, but the new cattle were castrated and branded, and without incident, to him anyway. The poor calves had been uneasy at being cordoned into a separate pen from their mothers, then grew increasingly terrified as they were marched into the narrow chute where they could be confined while they were cut and branded. Their bleating, and the smell of the burning hair and flesh, was something Nick could never quite get accustomed to, even having lived more than half of his life around them. The whiskey last night couldn't come soon enough.

Nick carried his coffee to the porch and watched the sun come up over the pastures. The freshly-cut hay was piled in shaggy mounds across the field; it smelled like green decay. The thought of it made his hand stray to the scar on his neck, and his mind drifted to the day he'd gotten it.

He'd been young, only eleven, playing around the hay barn with Josephine, clambering about in the loft in a bid to impress her. She'd already proved herself to be every bit as fast as him, so he had to rely on daredevilry to distinguish himself. In a final display of his prowess, he'd balanced on the very edge of the loft and posed, chin jutting out like the Scarlet Pimpernel. But it jutted too far, and he fell, down to where the horse-drawn hay mowers and sulky rakes were stored, an arsenal of cold steel blades.

Dozens of rusty curving tines punctured his clothes and skin like wet paper. The pain came from everywhere, so bright and searing that he was scared to move, lest he make it worse. He clearly remembered his throat filling with his blood, and the drowning sensation of being unable to breathe. And Josephine screaming. Screaming as loud as she could. Only stopping when she climbed down into the blades to get him out. The sharpened fingers tore at her too, blood streaming down her shoulder and arms as she struggled to pull him out. He didn't want to move, but she told him he had to, that he would die if he didn't. She had already got him free by the time the adults came running.

He passed out before they ever got him out of the barn. His next memory was looking up from his bed at a roomful of people. The doctor was tending to Josephine, who lay eyes-closed but alive in a cot beside his bed. The doctor's assistant was wringing out blood-soaked towels into a bucket, all the while watching Josephine with a look like hunger. When he saw Nicholas watching him, the old man struggled to lift the bucket and then limped awkwardly away with it. The rusty smell of blood lingered in the room even after the bucket had been carried out. The doctor was telling Nicholas's parents that he had never seen so much blood. If it hadn't been for Josephine, Nicholas would have surely died from the deep laceration on his throat. And that Nicholas owed her his life. He never forgot that. His hand lingered on the scar that made sure of it, even as a keening bird call snapped him back to the present.

Nick went back inside for a breakfast of eggs and home fries with Brandon, and then set out for home as soon as was polite. Brandon watched him go, yelling his thanks. Nick settled his horse into a brisk pace, anxious to see Josephine, and after a few miles his head began to feel better. As Josephine had predicted, Nick and Brandon had thrown back a few more drinks than was prudent last night. Coffee and sun and silence were as good a hangover cure as a Texan could hope for, and he had plenty of all three. Luckily he was already feeling better when his horse saw the snake.

The horse stopped instantly, almost throwing him, and began backing up and snorting. The rattlesnake was midsize, about four feet long, and had been sunning itself in the middle of the trail. Nick calmed the horse and reached in his pocket for the revolver. But by the time he'd gotten his hand on the grip, the snake had already begun its unconcerned slither off to the side of the trail. Nick cocked the hammer and sighted at it. His instinct as a rancher was to kill any snake he saw, especially rattlers. But something stayed his hand. The snake was minding its own business, not climbing into his boots or anything; he was the interloper here. No reason to kill something just because you could. He contemplated firing into the air, just for a sense of release. But it would spook the already tense horse, and it certainly wouldn't help his headache. Sometimes being an adult meant suppressing your vital urges. Or at least postponing them.

The scrubby landscape of mesquite and stunted pines finally gave way to the rocky hills of Austin by midmorning, and Nick picked up the pace. When he saw bluebonnets by the road, it occurred to him to pick a few. Before he had laid a hand on one, Brandon's voice came back to him from last night, after the third whiskey: "You know there's no future with her, no matter how much she winds you up…"

Nick had at first tried to pretend he didn't know Brandon meant Josephine, but Brandon wasn't hearing it. He turned his face as serious as three whiskeys would allow. "Nick, I've known you my whole life, and I've seen you two together. Maybe you think nobody notices, but everybody notices." Nick sat up straight and his face fell into a scowl, but Brandon kept on, slurring slightly: "Look, she's a cute girl, and y'all have a lot of history. But sooner or later, you're going to have to marry somebody, a white girl, and carry on the family name. Out here you might get away with what you're thinking of, but in prim-and-goddamned-proper Austin, the state capital for Christ's sake, that ain't gonna fly. I'm telling you this as your friend. Your mother turns to ice every time she sees you talking to Josephine. One time she had me cornered and I had to listen to her whole 'the red bird doesn't fly with the black bird' speech." Brandon punctuated the memory with a loud belch. "I wouldn't be surprised if she got rid of the girl when you're not around to defend her."

Nick had thought of an angry and profane retort, but in the end had slouched back into the leather slung chair and sighed. Brandon was right and he knew it. It had put a melancholy pall on the evening, right up until Brandon retold the story of how he'd unintentionally wound up "married" in Mexico, and had to ride for his life to get away single. When Brandon got to the part about galloping through the cacti with no pants on, his laughter was irresistible, no matter how many times Nick had heard the story.

Nick gathered a handful of bluebonnets and got back on his way. When he turned down the packed earth of

Guadalupe Street, he saw the proud Raeburn home among the rows of equally ostentatious houses. There was activity in front of the house. Unfamiliar horses were tied out front.

As he approached, one of the cooks called out, "It's Mr. Nick!" She ran out to meet him and started blurting out words without pausing to breathe. "The man came again last night – Count Lune. He took Josephine! She's gone, and there's blood all in her room!"

Nick jumped from the horse, tossed the reins to the cook, and ran for the house. He found his mother sitting in the parlor with a policeman. She looked up at Nick with eyes red-rimmed as if from tears, but angry. "It's just terrible, Nicholas," she began. "He broke in the window and came into our house. He could've killed any of us, or all of us!" She turned to the policeman and said, "He must be stopped. We pay good money for the police force. What good is it when horrible people can just come into a prominent house with no repercussions?"

The officer started a flustered reply, when Nick interrupted: "Mother, what happened? Alice said Josephine is gone. Did anyone see anything?" When she didn't answer, he added, "Was anyone else hurt?"

Nick's mother turned to him. "No, no one else is hurt. Someone broke into Josephine's window. One of the men heard a commotion outside, but not in time to catch him. There's blood all over her room."

To the policeman, she said, "Can you give us a minute please?" and walked into the dining room, beckoning Nick to follow her. She closed the door behind him.

"Nicholas, I know Josephine means something to you, but I have to know: why did this man come back for her again? Why not someone else? The police say he's never gone back to the same house twice before. Is she involved with something? Is she drawing this man to us? You need to tell me."

Nick's instinct was to defend Josephine and attack his mother in kind. But it was too much to take in; he wasn't on firm enough mental footing to argue. And he really didn't know the answer. Why would the man come back? Especially after ten years? And with all the precautions they'd taken – the fence, the dog... He sighed. "I don't know, Mother. I really don't. I don't think Josephine is involved with anything. But I have no idea what attracts this man." His mind raced, thinking of what he should do, of how to find her. His mother watched him wordlessly. He added, "Are you alright, Mother? Can I help you with the police?"

His mother snorted. "I don't need help with them, but they might need help with me if they don't start protecting the good people of this town!" With that, she rushed back into the parlor, reinvigorated with a fresh batch of righteous indignation. Nick hurried to Josephine's room.

With a slow survey, he took in the room. Seeing the glass and blood on the floor made his throat tighten at the thought of her being hurt. He squatted for a better view of the mess on the floor, and spotted something white under the edge of the bed. He reached under and retrieved an antler-handled knife ... the one he'd given her after she'd been attacked the first time. Her name was engraved in the handle in flowing cursive. There was blood on the blade, and that made him catch his breath. Blood on her knife might mean the blood on the floor was the attacker's, not hers. It was enough to give Nick some hope, some strength to keep moving forward.

He heard the door creak behind him, and turned to see the face of the cook peering in. At his glance, she started to withdraw, but Nick called out, "Wait." She came back. "Who saw them?" Nick asked. "Or heard anything? I need to talk to them."

"We all heard the dog barking," she said. "Andrew went

outside to see. Then he started yelling, and told us to stay inside."

Nick nodded. "When you saw me in the street, you said 'Count Lune' had taken her. What does that mean?"

She cast her eyes to the floor. "That's just who they say he is," she said sheepishly. Then seeing Nick's unwavering, questioning stare, she added, "Some of the help in town call him that."

Nick's face softened, seeing how frightened she was. "Thank you. Are you alright?"

"Yes, just worried about Josephine, and what he's gonna do to her." Nick's breath caught at that, and his guts clenched like he might vomit. She hastily added, "I'm sorry," and left him alone.

Nick stood up and walked to the kitchen, where the rest of the household was gathered. He found Andrew, a tall young man with exhaustion written around his eyes. Nick pulled out a chair and motioned for Andrew to sit, and then crouched in front of him.

"Can you tell me what you saw?"

"Yes, sir." Andrew nodded. "When I went out to check on Fausto, I saw someone moving in the yard. I hollered out but nobody answered. So I got the lantern and went out there. The man was going out through a hole in the fence, dragging Miss Josephine behind him. The dog was acting crazy, trying to bite him, then running around, then biting again. I went out to them, but when I got close my head hurt real bad, and I couldn't see good. I thought the lantern was going out, but it was fine. I just couldn't see." He grabbed at the cross he wore around his neck and muttered something under his breath. "They was already on his horse when Jacob ran out and fired a shot over him, but the man didn't stop."

"Would you be able to recognize the man if you saw him again?"

"No sir, I couldn't ever rightly see him." He looked around at the others in the kitchen before going on, as if waiting for approval. "But I know who might." Nick was aware of a few of the onlookers whispering to each other.

"What do you mean?"

"That stuff with my eyes and my head... That's voodoo." He looked around again. "And if he's using voodoo, then Mama Queenie knows about it."

Nick scowled in disgust. This was a real kidnapping, not some superstitious boogeyman bullshit. He started to rebuke the boy but realized this was truly all he had to go on. Nick didn't believe in voodoo, but if the man that took Josephine believed in it, then this might be the path to her. "Alright, where can I find this Mama Queenie?"

Andrew looked up in surprise, apparently not expecting that answer. He didn't know an address, but he told Nick what streets to go down to find her. Nick thanked him and went back to the parlor, where the weather-beaten policeman continued to attempt to pacify Nick's mother. Nick interrupted: "Excuse me, but the cook's helper... the one who saw the man, thinks you should interview a Mama Queenie."

The officer snorted and shook his head. "If I had a nickel... We can't chase down every fairy tale that frightens somebody. When I need a love potion I'll see Mama Queenie. When I want to catch a killer, I use modern police methods. We will collect evidence and interview witnesses." The officer stood and nodded to Nick and his mother. "We will catch this man. Have no doubt."

But will you do it in time to save Josephine, wondered Nick. He started to reply that this man had eluded the police for ten years, but he held his tongue. Maybe they would catch him. But Nick couldn't just wait idly and hope. That's not what Josephine would've done for him.

* * *

It was early afternoon by the time Nick made it to Mama Queenie's place of business, a laundry on the east side of Austin. The small wooden buildings on this street seemed a world away from the opulent new stone edifices around the capitol. The exterior of the laundry was trim and neat, the siding recently painted a pale blue. But inside Nick found a jam-packed, run-down ramshackle affair. There weren't any signs of clothes being washed. It had more in common with a dry-goods store, or an herbalist, or maybe a butcher. It reeked of cardamom and exotic scents he couldn't identify.

The long main room had a wood-topped service counter at one end, and two chairs at the other. Lining the walls were shelves packed with leaves, stems, roots. Mason jars held soil or liquids, and a few shelves seemed devoted to dried or drying carcasses of rabbits, squirrels, birds, and a number of creatures of indeterminate origin. A large man sat in a chair in the corner, his skin so dark it was hard to make out his expression in the sparse light. He was in hunched conversation with an old Mexican woman, but he paused to eye Nicholas. A child played with a doll on the floor near them. Nicholas cleared his throat and said to no one in particular, "Excuse me, I'm looking for Mama Queenie."

The large man looked up at him but didn't speak. He glanced back toward a bead curtain behind the counter, then turned his attention back to his companion. Nick wasn't sure what to do next.

Presently a woman, hunched into near shapelessness in the way older women can get, came shuffling out through the curtain. She wore a faded red cotton smock, at odds with the bright blue bandana that covered her head.

"Are you Mama Queenie?" Nick ventured.

"That depend. Are you the tax man?" the woman answered. Her thin voice had an odd rise and fall that reminded Nick of the Caribbean.

Nick tried to stammer that he was not, but the large man threw back his head and let out a squawking laugh like a seagull.

"What kind of thing can I help you with?" she asked.

Nick leaned across the counter and spoke quietly, "I'm..." He hesitated because his voice was breaking, then rushed through it: "I'm looking for the man who takes the girls."

Mama Queenie inhaled sharply, sucking air around dark brown teeth. "Everybody looking for that man. What makes you think I can help you?"

"I was told he, uh... uses voodoo, and that you would know about it."

"All I know is that you need to walk your narrow ass out of my place, and if I have to ask twice, Joseph will help you out." She nodded at the large man in the corner, who was no longer laughing. She began to turn back toward the curtain, muttering, "I don't know you from Adam, and you think..."

Nick exclaimed, "Wait! I have to find this man. He's taken Josephine!"

"And what is she to you?" Mama Queenie asked. She hadn't turned back to Nick, but she hadn't gone through the curtain either.

Nick stammered, "She's... she's my..." He stopped. What was she? "She saved my life. I owe her my life."

Mama Queenie turned and looked him square in the face, considering him, and one eyebrow crept up. Finally, she leaned her bulk across the counter and said in hushed tones, "This man you looking for, he's not hard to find. You just be sure you want to find him when you go looking for him. I might tell you some things, but I can't help you here. And if I can't help you here, I don't need anyone seeing you here. Bad for business. You come to my house tonight." She reached under the counter and tore a scrap of paper off of a wrapped bundle. "I'm going to draw you a map. 'Cause I don't need you wandering around asking directions to my house either." She scrawled a few intersecting lines and scribbled some street names with a feather quill, then handed the paper to him. She waddled back toward the doorway.

"What time should I be there?" Nick asked.

"You wait 'til it's good and dark, like a moth with no wings." And she disappeared without another word.

* * *

Just after dark, Nick set out for the address on the paper. It was far south and east of the capitol, well past the erstwhile laundry. By the time the electric streetcar reached the end of its run, he was the last remaining white passenger. As he continued on foot, he consciously kept his head down, trying not to draw attention to himself as he followed the map. But as he rounded the corner onto Chalmers Street, voices shouting in excitement brought his head up.

A crowd was gathered around the smoldering ruins of a house. The blackened remains of the walls stood up like gnarled teeth. Nick looked at his map and confirmed what he already feared: the smoking building was his destination. He looked around in despair, and began to reach out to the nearest person to ask what happened, when he heard his name called. The sound came from a house across the street. He crossed the road and approached the darkened porch, where he saw a large person sitting on a chair, covered in a red blanket. The voice, he now realized, was Mama Queenie's. He didn't recall ever telling her his name.

"If you want to tell the whole world you here, you done it, coming in here like a one-leg bird. Might as well sit on down. They gonna be a while. You can't put that fire out with plain water."

Nick asked, "What happened? Are you alright?"

Mama Queenie said, "This afternoon I was like a cow pissing on a flat rock, didn't know if I should help you or not.

Didn't really wanna rile up a lot of trouble. Didn't need to invite him to come after me. But now he's come after me anyway, so I won't be keeping any secrets for him."

"He did this? The man who takes the girls? Count Lune?" After a moment of realization, he said, "Just because you talked to me in the store?"

"You don't really want to be saying that name, you follow? I'll say *he* made this happen. And since he didn't get me, I'd say he's weak. Getting your girl must've taken a bunch out of him. Maybe near used him up."

"Who is he? Just tell me how I can find him, and I'll have him arrested."

Mama Queenie snorted at that. "This ain't a man you going to arrest. If the policemen and the Pinkerton detectives wanted to find the man, they might find him. But they might know better, too. They might just want to arrest enough people to make everybody feel safe, and hope this man stops taking the girls on his own."

Nick didn't know what to say. It was preposterous. He didn't believe for a second that the police were afraid of this man. But he wasn't here to argue, he was here for information. "I have to find him. How do I do that?"

Mama Queenie leaned back and took a thoughtful breath. "I don't rightly know his real name, or where he's staying."

He couldn't believe it. She was wasting his time. Was this some kind of bait-and-switch? A ploy to get him to buy a voodoo potion?

Mama Queenie went on: "But I can tell you what to look for. I know this man since I was younger. Young as you. He come to me back then, wanting to learn about the art and the ceremony. Wanting to learn to be a vodu himself. He was serious, this man. Practiced everything I taught him like his life depended on it. So I helped him, but he always wanted more. I finally found out why he was so desperate." She stopped and looked around, as if someone might be listening. "That boy did something bad wrong, and he didn't want to go to hell for it. He was looking for some way to avoid his fate, or at least postpone it. I showed him what I could, but it wasn't enough for him. After I told him I wouldn't truck with that side of things, I didn't see him no more. But I hear about him. I hear rustlings in the spirit world, him communicating with powerful shades. And I hear stories about him in the physical world too. Traveling round, buying up artifacts. Messing with things better left alone." She shook her head in disapproval.

"How do you know this is the same man? That must've been…" Nick tried to put this delicately: "…decades ago."

"Oh, it's the same man. He leaves a… taste on his works." She spat on the floor. "He's been doing this for, like you say, decades. It's dealing with these forces that lets him live this long. Our voodoo, what we do round here, the love potions and charms, we dealing with local spirits, people that was born here and died here. What this man is doing, he talking to older forces, ones that ain't from around here. He's killing these girls to get the attention of these forces. Years ago, when he killed all those girls, the spirits paid him attention. But then they stopped, and he's been getting desperate, I've heard. Now, he must think he's got a way to attract them again."

"He came for her before, back then," Nick said. "Almost ten years ago."

"And that tells us something, doesn't it?" She nodded her head and narrowed her eyes. "It means he ain't just taking the first girl he sees like a jackdaw. The girls he takes are special. He's marked these girls somehow, tied them to himself, so they garner more attention in the darkest places."

"Alright, but how do I find him?"

"You do persist, don't you?" Mama Queenie sighed. "I

make sure I don't know where he live. It would be bad for me. But if I was looking, I'd be looking for a house with a big yard. What he's got to be doing is going to take cooking up herbs and singing the songs. It'll be louder than newlyweds, and he won't want anybody living too close by."

Useless, thought Nick. A vague description that could apply to half the houses in Austin. Just like a carnival fortuneteller. She was playing games with him. He shook his head in frustration.

Mama Queenie continued like she hadn't noticed: "On his roof he's gonna have a cat with wings. He probably have the same things at the corners of his yard. That's his icon, always was. Those'll be keeping watch over his *abode*. And his front door is gonna have tall mirrors on either side of it. Probably be a white door. That's how you know him. And I can tell you the name he used back when he came to me. He used to be Leon Principe. He may call himself something different now, but it might be close to that. What you make people call you gives you juju." She smiled wryly at this last bit, and Nick thought about what people called *her*.

Maybe he'd judged her too quickly. It might be all horseshit, but it was at least provable. As a man of science, he valued a hypothesis that could be tested, and this description was a pretty good start. Thinking the interview was over, he reached for his wallet. "Thank you very much. How much do I owe you?"

Mama Queenie held both hands in front of her in a warding gesture. "I won't be taking any of your money for that information, I can tell you that. But I'm not done with you anyway. If I'm going to send you in there, I might as well tell you what to look for. If you find the girl, you get her and yourself away from him. Don't you think you're gonna fight this man. Unless he lying on the ground with his eyes closed, you run. You won't be able to kill him. But he's an old man, and weakened. He can't strike you down with lightning or any of the other fool things they've been saying in town. If he could, he already would've tried it on me, instead of this…" She swept her large arm toward the smoking shell of her house. "But if you can spill his blood, you do it."

"I thought you said not to fight him," Nick said.

"I don't mean cut his body. He may have some of his blood in containers, or in talismans. He used to wear an ankh around his neck before, with his blood inside it. Looks like a stick figure with no legs, made out of clay. And he might have his blood in a clay pot. If you can break these things, it will weaken him more. You spill it on the ground, not down a sink or in water, you understand? Pour it on the bare earth. Might even weaken him enough that other things will come to help you. There are beings that he owes debts to, that stalk him. His power keeps him hidden from them, but if his blood touches the earth, they can find him." She pursed her lips in thought. "And don't tell him your real name if you can help it," she concluded. "But that's probably already a lost cause." She reached into her dress and pulled out an amulet on a cord, a round disk that looked like a sun. She muttered something, maybe in French, moving the amulet in a clockwise circle.

"What was that for?"

"I'm asking Papa Legba to protect the foolish," she said, looking at Nicholas. "Both of us."

"Would carrying something like that, uh, protect me?" He felt embarrassed before the words even cleared his mouth.

"No," said Mama Queenie, wagging her head in disappointment. "You not a believer. It would just be a waste, might even angry them up. Best you just depend on your young bones and your wits." She smiled again. He wasn't sure if that was meant to be a joke or not.

* * *

Capturing the girl had taken a huge toll on him, much more than he was prepared for. Especially the loss of blood from her damnable knife. He had already used up so much of it in his preparations, to lose more in the actual kidnapping was severely depleting, almost life-threatening. But he had her, he finally had her, one of his lost children.

When he'd gotten her back to his house, he'd had just enough strength left to blindfold her and bind her wrists behind her to the leg of a table. Then he'd collapsed in his bed. He wasn't sure how long he slept, but he awoke to the sound of her screaming. He hobbled down the stairs from his bedroom, shivering and leaning heavily on the banister and his walking stick. He shielded his eyes from the high sun as he entered the plant-filled room he thought of as his laboratory. The usually soothing atmosphere of the greenhouse was totally spoiled by her shrieks. As he got closer, the screaming became harder to bear. There were no words, just a high ragged wail punctuated by her gasping breaths.

"Stop it!" he shouted. Either she couldn't hear him over her screams, or she didn't care. She left him no choice. He pushed aside the trailing red leaves of a bromeliad on the table and slapped her across the face. That stopped her. She flung her head back and forth searchingly. Her unkempt kinky hair had worked partly free of its braids, and her nightgown was badly torn where it rode up her dark bare legs. She was tied and blindfolded, but now it seemed a gag might be required too.

Maybe not, maybe she could be reasonable.

"If you don't stop screaming, I'm going to gag you," he said, his voice a low growl. "Are you going to scream again?"

She turned her head toward the sound of his voice, seeming to look for him. "What do you want? Why are you doing this?" she demanded, sobbing.

He chuckled. "Why am I doing this? I don't think anything I could say would explain it to you. Not in a way you would understand. You're much too young. I'm sorry, dear, I truly am. But I have to make an audience with the masters, and you are the price of admission. I wish it were different, but I don't make the rules."

"What are you talking about? You kill girls! I know who you are. You killed them, and you tried to kill me. Just let me go!" She arched her back and pulled against the table leg, but it didn't budge. She slouched down, sobbing. "There aren't rules. Just let me go. Please let me go!" Her voice rose into screaming again. "Please let me go!"

He pulled a strip of cloth from the table she was tied to and bent down to tie it around her open mouth, thinking how similar this was to tying a tomato plant up to a stake. As he drew close to her, she must've heard his breathing, and kicked out with her bare foot. The blow caught his bad right leg and he fell to one knee, gripping her shoulder to keep himself from falling. The girl immediately turned her head and bit down on his wrist, incisors breaking the skin and seeking for bone. He tore his hand away, rolling backward onto the ground. His wrist bled freely, soaking the shirtsleeve.

The pain in his wrist and his leg battled for attention as he haltingly regained his feet. But his groan of effort turned to rasping laughter when he saw the blood running down her lower lip. "You might be worth the effort yet, little bitch. Even with all my preparations, I never imagined I'd get you to willingly ingest my blood." She swung her head wildly, trying to push the blindfold off with her shoulder, and punctuated her renewed screaming with spitting. He drew the walking stick back, the heavy silver figure of the winged cat at its top sweeping behind his head, and then brought it down on Josephine's temple. Her noises died in a grunt, and new blood crept slowly from her forehead to mingle with his on her chin.

* * *

Wednesday, May 8th, 1895

The electric streetcars had already shut down for the night when Nick had left Mama Queenie last night, so he'd been relegated to the slow plod of the mule-driven trolleys. He'd used the time to think of how to go about finding the house. Sleep had been fitful, and he'd been extremely distracted in his morning physics class, not realizing until the class laughed that'd he'd started to read the same page of notes twice.

After class, he'd skipped his scheduled office hours and gone straight to the post office. There, after some forced smalltalk and the pointed use of his family name, he'd been allowed to study the Austin Postal Register. He hadn't found anyone named Principe, but did find a Princeps. His memory of classical languages was enough to realize that both meant "prince," the former in Spanish, the latter in Latin. His address was west of downtown, on Crockett Street, and Nick set out immediately.

When he reached the address, near the railroad track, he found a beige limestone house set well back from the street. It was surrounded by a black wrought-iron fence that connected to tall brick columns at each corner. On top of each column was a black, wrought figure of a winged animal. Anyone casually passing by might mistake it for an eagle, or maybe Pegasus. However, on careful inspection the animal was a cat, sitting with its birdlike wings outstretched, its mouth wide open in what appeared to be a scream. Looking up, Nick saw that the elaborate weathervane on the roof featured a similar figure, this one standing on all fours, with its mouth closed. It struck Nick how little attention he paid to these things. He was sure his own house had a weathervane on the roof, and he could not for the life of him recall what sort of animal was depicted. A rooster or a lion, maybe?

The house showed no signs of anyone being home, nor did the houses on either side. The neighboring houses, in fact, both showed signs of neglect – unkempt lawns and peeling paint – as if they might be uninhabited. Now that he had found a house that fit Mama Queenie's description, he realized he didn't have any kind of actual plan, no idea what to do next. He'd envisioned himself watching the house, hoping to catch sight of the owner leaving. But failing this, he supposed he was going to march up to the front door, confront whoever this person was, and barge right in and rescue Josephine. What else was there to do? Call on the police and tell them he'd found a house with cat gargoyles and that an old voodoo woman said this meant it was the kidnapper's house?

He stood at the gate and pivoted to look up the street in both directions. The motion made the revolver in his coat pocket bang against his hip; the substantial weight comforted him. This was Texas, by God! He'd let Samuel Colt do his talking for him.

He reached out to the embellished iron gateway that barred the front walkway. A simple clasp held it closed, and it opened easily. Nick stuck his right hand into his pocket and felt the cool heft of the revolver grip. He moved cautiously up the length of the walkway, landscaped on both sides with a variety of bushy plants that he didn't recognize, bright and lush, like something out of a Paul Gaugin painting. They looked like they needed more water than what fell in central Texas. Someone was taking special care of them.

He climbed the stone steps onto the small front porch. Just as Mama Queenie had said, the door was flanked by tall narrow mirrors, but the door itself was black, not white. Nick hesitated, looking again at the street. He was quite alone. He placed his ear to the door. Nothing. Finally, he knocked. There was no response. He knocked again and replaced his ear on the door. He heard no signs of movement inside. Now what? He stepped backwards to see if any windows were left open. On impulse, he grabbed the doorknob. It turned and the door swung inward.

Well, I guess that makes sense, Nick thought. If he's Count Lune, who's going to break into his house?

Just thinking the name conjured an image of Josephine. What was this man doing to her? He stepped quickly through the door and closed it behind him.

Inside, it was dark and hot and silent. There was a scent of pungent herbs, not unlike Mama Queenie's store. As his eyes adjusted, he saw that he was in a parlor that seemed disused. Formal furniture with faded fabric sat on an oriental rug. A thin layer of dust coated most of the surfaces. The shades were drawn and admitted very little light. He considered calling out, but decided he might as well preserve whatever element of surprise he had. He froze when he heard a low rustling coming from deeper in the house. At the far end of a long hall, he saw faint light spilling from under a closed door.

Nick padded toward the door as quietly as he could, but the bare wood floor tried its best to announce him. He crept around the base of the central staircase and came to a doorway to his left. Slowly, he peered around its threshold to find a formal dining room, similarly neglected. He moved past it to the hall's end and cautiously pushed open the swinging door. Behind it was the kitchen, brightly lit by unshaded windows and showing signs of recent use. Clean dishes were still damp and stacked in the drying rack by the sink.

Nick fell into a crouch as he heard the rustling sound again, louder, and noises that might be voices. The sounds stopped, and Nick crept to the back of the kitchen to find the source. Glass French doors looked into a world of dense greenery dappled with sunlight. Nick stood against the wall to the side of the doors and peeked through the glass. It was so bright inside that it was hard to make out detail, but he saw no movement, and the sounds did not return. After a moment of hesitation, he decided that surprise was half the battle, and pushed through the doors with the gun held out in front of him.

He nearly stumbled on the two steps that led him down to the packed dirt floor of some kind of greenhouse. The rustling noise started again, louder and closer, and Nick swung the revolver toward it, unable to see well in the dazzling light. He found himself pointing a gun at two brightly-colored caged birds. Their large wire enclosure stood at Nick's eye level. They flapped their wings and tilted their heads while they looked at him. After a moment, they relaxed and sat still, watching him. A quick survey of the room showed no other animate things, but what must be hundreds of plants. Three walls were mostly windows; skylights admitted sunlight from above. The air was hot and moist, fecund, with the bright smells of blooming things and the deep scents of fertile soil and decaying leaves. He had to cover his mouth to prevent a sneeze.

Plants lined the back edges of potting tables around all three exterior walls such that he could barely see out. Every inch of the tables that didn't hold plants held a bizarre array of paraphernalia: dowsing rods, a microscope, small carved figures both beautiful and profane, colorful beads strung together as bracelets and necklaces, feathers and bones and stacks of small lidded glass jars containing powders and liquids. In the center of the room was a table with a galvanized metal top, an office chair in front of it. This table, too, held jars, but also papers in stacks and jumbled piles, books slumping diagonally on each other, and cups of pens and pencils. In the middle, something familiar caught his eye and made his pulse pound: the long thin leather knife sheath with Josephine's initials stamped on it. This was the place, there was no doubt. This was Count Lune's house; he'd brought her here.

Nick gripped the pistol tighter.

He crouched and examined the floor, seeing signs of recent and vigorous activity. Fresh ruts led from the door to the nearest table, as if something had been dragged. In front of that table were scratch marks, sliding shoeprints, and the prints of bare feet and hands; plus damp puddles and spatters of something dark, maybe blood. From this vantage, he saw something odd on the other side of the table: a low stone pedestal of some sort, like a small altar. On its front and side were crude carvings of humans and animals and creatures that blurred the boundaries between them. On the top were circles of multicolored wax drippings, where two candles had obviously burned for quite a long time. But no candles stood there now.

She had been in this room. He had to find her, and soon. This man did not go after girls to keep them. He did horrible things to them, and then killed them. He had killed seven already, and Nick was not going to let Josephine be the eighth.

Nick rushed out of the room, back into the front parlor, trying to see if he'd missed anything. He'd seen all of the downstairs of the house. He cocked an ear up the stairs. Not hearing anything, he bounded up, taking them two at a time. At the top of the landing were three doorways, all open. The first was a large bedroom that held a wardrobe and the various bric-a-brac of being lived in. The other two were smaller bedrooms, neither of which showed any signs of recent use. Nothing; no one here. He went back downstairs and did another circuit of the rooms. He hadn't missed any doors; there was no one here. He'd learned nothing; it was a dead end.

He went back into the greenhouse room, the only place he'd found anything helpful. This time the birds ignored him. He pushed aside the chair and looked down at the desk. Was there more here? Many of the books were in languages he didn't read; some he didn't even recognize. The ones in English had titles like *Herbal Remedies* and *The Wisdom of the Native People*.

He picked up the knife sheath. The two cotton laces Josephine used to tie it around her ankle had been cut, not untied. Nick didn't like that at all. Under the sheath he saw a fancy envelope, opened. It seemed familiar. It looked like the one his mother had shown him, the invitation to the moontower lighting. Turning the paper over, it bore the state seal of Texas. Inside was an invitation for Dr. Princeps to attend the moonlight tower dedication. Nick started to place the envelope back on top of the stack, but the papers below it caught his eye.

It was a disorderly pile of newspaper clippings. Riffling through them, he saw that most were from the *Austin Weekly Statesman*, and were mainly concerned with the funding, installation, and impending dedication of the moontowers. Some detailed Austin's purchase of the towers from Detroit, which was getting rid of them. Others thanked the generosity of the wealthy Austinites who had made the purchase possible. A corner of one paper from lower in the stack stood apart from the rest. The paper stock was a different shade, the text in a different typeface. This one had a handwritten note in the margin. Nick looked more closely at the article, which proved to be from the *Detroit Free Press*, an opinion piece advocating the removal of the huge light towers. It mentioned the ugliness of the towers and their harsh, glaring light. A later paragraph was circled in ink. It concerned how unnatural this nighttime illumination was, and the bizarre and frightening effects it was having, that chickens and other fowl, not knowing when to sleep, were dying of exhaustion. That pedestrians found themselves confused and dazed by the unnatural aspects of the illumination. A hand-drawn arrow from this text led to the note scrawled in the margin:

"Just as we have hoped, They are attracted to the unnaturally bright lights at night, and Their attention on the surrounding populace can be felt even by those not studied in the Arts. A renewed time of communication with the Oldest Ones is upon us! You must do whatever is necessary to bring these lights to Austin!"

Nick put the paper back on the pile, going over it in his mind. There was nothing here that helped him find Josephine, but it was apparent that Princeps had an abiding interest in the moontower dedication. In the absence of any other leads, Nick would have to track Princeps down there.

Nick snorted, realizing that his mother had gotten what she wanted. Nick would be attending the debut after all.

But how would Nick recognize Princeps? He looked around the cluttered table for some kind of portrait. The best he could do was a glossy handout from the city. The inside contained a map of the thirty-one tower locations, two of which had been circled in red ink. The back of the leaflet included a group photo of some well-dressed older people; the caption thanked the generous donors, including Mrs. Marie Raeburn and a Dr. Leon Princeps. But the people were standing in a disorganized mass, so it wasn't clear which one he was. Nick stuffed the brochure in his jacket; it might at least help narrow down who he was looking for.

He looked up at the clock sitting on the table. Only 6:30? He glanced at his own pocket watch to confirm. Plenty of time to make it to the dedication by 8:00. He turned to leave, but something nagged at his attention. A braided silk cord was looped over the face of the old clock, and hanging from it was a looped cross, an Egyptian ankh. It was thick and made of clay, its surface painted in wavy stripes in lurid reds and blues. Was this the talisman Mama Queenie had told him about? In his rush, he had totally forgotten about it. Whether it was the right thing or not, Nick decided it was coming with him. He pocketed it and strode out the door.

He was quite a ways from downtown, but if he could catch a streetcar he'd be home with ample time to figure out which of his dinner jackets hid a pistol the best.

* * *

The white portion of the Raeburn household disembarked from the hired carriage at 7:45 pm, at the entrance to Hyde Park. Nick's mother, Marie, led the procession, chin outthrust, shoulders back, nose firmly in the air. She took no notice of the dozens of children, black and white, running around the park, chasing each other in and out of the shadows and screaming in exhilaration at being allowed to play this long after bedtime.

The outer edges of the grassy park were covered with picnic blankets strewn like flower petals. Families ate by the light of candles. In the middle of the clearing was the moontower itself. It was impossible not to gaze up at it — a tall skeletal structure of gray metal bars that reached up over a hundred feet into the darkness. It looked improbably thin to support the bulk of the six arc lights arranged around a hexagon at its top. At the base of the structure was a temporary wooden stage; in front of this was a cluster of formal tables with white tablecloths and silver centerpieces in the shape of miniature moontowers.

Nick's mother led the way toward the stage and was intercepted by a waiter in a dark suit. Upon hearing her name, he ushered the group to a table to the left of the stage. There they found name cards for each of them. Nick quickly read all of the cards at their table, looking for Princeps, but not finding it. He noted his mother doing the same. He started to check the cards at the empty tables nearby, when she called him back.

"Nicholas, these are the Wagners I've been telling you about," she said, indicating placards at their table. "They have two lovely daughters, Cynthia and Stephanie I believe. I'd be surprised if any of the finer girls don't have an escort already, but it can't hurt to introduce yourself."

"Yes, of course," said Nick absently, scanning the crowd. "I'll just be a moment. I think I see someone from the university." Nick walked along all the tables, reading the names as he went. At the third table he saw "Dr. L. Princeps." The chair had a dark topcoat and scarf draped over it. Nick's pulse quickened. So Princeps was here. Now Nick just had to find him.

The problem was that Nick still didn't know what Princeps looked like. Every man here was dressed nearly identically, in some variety of dark three-piece suit. Even the sheriff had dressed up for the occasion. After a quick search, Nick located the waiter who had seated them. Nick pulled a dollar out of his pocket as he approached. "Excuse me, I think you've seated Dr. Princeps. Do you know where he went?" Nick placed the coin in the man's hand. The waiter looked down at it with feigned disinterest.

"I believe that is Dr. Princeps there, speaking with Mayor Hancock." The waiter pointed with his chin, and then was gone, and the dollar with him.

Nick looked in the indicated direction, and watched two men in animated conversation laughing affably. Nick waited, accepting several shrimp from passing waiters, realizing he hadn't eaten since breakfast. The mayor was tall, handsome, and unmistakable, his slick hair parted meticulously in the middle. The man he spoke with was smaller, neatly dressed, and appeared to be very old. He carried a silver-topped cane and leaned heavily on it. Presently the mayor excused himself to speak to another potential voter. Nick immediately approached the older man, stuffing uneaten shrimp in his pocket as he went, realizing that he had no idea what he was going to say.

"Dr. Princeps?" he asked, unable to conceal a hint of accusation.

The older man looked up at him, and a slight smile curled the corners of his mouth. "I am. But I'm afraid you have me at a disadvantage, sir." His voice was low and hoarse, like that of a habitual smoker, and he spoke with the long vowels of South Texas. His silver hair was cut short and combed as precisely as his thin gray mustache.

"I know who you are and what you do at night," Nick began in a low voice. "I know you took Josephine. Tell me where she is," Nick demanded, a bit surprised at the vehemence of the words coming out of his mouth.

Princeps seemed nonplussed, but the slight smile never left his face. "You must have me confused with someone else, sir. I haven't the faintest idea what you're talking about."

Nick was not going to be put off. "I've been to your house. I found her knife sheath there. If you won't tell me where she is, maybe you'll tell the police."

The bemused look fell from Princeps' face like a mask, replaced by a pursed mouth and tightening around his suddenly very alert and glaring eyes. He glanced at the people nearby and spoke quietly: "So you're the one who violated my house? You don't realize what you're meddling with, boy," he said, spitting the last word. "The police? What will you tell them? That you broke into a respectable old man's home and found what, a piece of leather? And if they believed you, what makes you think they would be able to extract information from me? Do you think I fear anything on this mortal plane?" He waved his hand dismissively at their surroundings.

Before Nick could respond, Princeps leaned very close to him. "Whoever led you to me, and I know who that was, should have prepared you better. The girl is already lost to you. When the moontowers ignite tonight, the girl will meet the only authorities I acknowledge. Unfortunately, she won't survive this meeting." His nostrils flared as he finished. "You'd best return to your mother and your fine house, Mr. Raeburn. Enjoy the rest of your evening, and the rest of your life. And pray that you never find yourself between me and what I want." Princeps turned and hobbled toward the tables.

Nick's heart raced, his jaw clenched as he fought the urge to go after Princeps, to grab him and beat the truth out of him. But he stopped himself and thought about what Princeps had said: Josephine was still alive. And Princeps had just admitted that he was going to kill her when the towers lit up. That was enough to tell the police. Now they'd have to listen to him. Even if they wouldn't arrest Princeps, they could at least delay his plans. The lights would only be on for ninety minutes tonight; it had been in the papers. Surely they could detain Princeps for that long. In fact, the sheriff was here somewhere right now. Nick turned in place, looking all around for the sheriff.

When Nick heard the sound of cutlery tapping a glass, calling for attention, he looked to the stage. The mayor was standing there next to a large map of Austin that showed the locations of the Moonlight Towers as bright beacons. He was smiling, waiting for the many conversations to die down. Nick returned to scanning the crowd, looking for the sheriff's trademark mustache. But his gaze caught on something else. Princeps wasn't in his seat, and his topcoat was gone. Nick cast around frantically. Finally, he saw the retreating back of a small old man with a cane hobbling toward the west side of the park. Nick glanced back at the crowd, searching desperately for the sheriff, but he knew it was hopeless. If he lost Princeps now, he might not find him again in time, police or no police. Nick had to stay with him.

"Fellow Austinites," the mayor's voice rang out. "It brings me great pleasure to see you all here on this auspicious evening when we usher Austin to the forefront of the electrical age!"

He paused to acknowledge polite clapping.

Nick shouldered through the crowd of people that were trying to reach their seats, and lost sight of the old man over a small hillock. He pushed people aside with both hands, swimming against the current of Austin's old money, ignoring the resulting protests.

The mayor continued: "Tonight we begin a new era where the beauty and safety of a full moon can be spread across the city, every night!"

When Nick broke free of the tide of dark suits and reached the hill himself, he saw Princeps had untied a black horse and climbed astride it. The horse was already trotting away south, and Nick changed direction to cut through the corner of the park, hoping to intercept him at the south entrance. But when Nick emerged onto Congress Street, the horse was a block ahead of him and quickly increasing the gap.

Nick pursued them for two blocks, until his lungs were aching. He slowed to a jog, panting. Not knowing what else to do, he yelled, "Stop! STOP!"

As he doubled over to catch his breath, he heard a man's voice from the middle of the street: "Friend, are you getting on or what?"

Nick looked up to see an electric streetcar stopped next to him, the conductor and several passengers looking down at him expectantly. The car was headed south. Nick jumped on, digging a nickel out of his pocket for the conductor.

The car lurched toward downtown. Nick remained standing at the front, disregarding the annoyed looks from the driver. Clutching a rail for balance, Nick craned his neck, looking for a sign of the horseman, but saw nothing. His mind raced. Princeps had mentioned meeting with someone when the lights came on. Why was that familiar? The newspaper clipping at Princeps' house... the scribbled note had said the moontowers themselves attracted some kind of beings. And Mama Queenie had said Count Lune was sacrificing the girls to make a deal with powerful beings. So, Princeps must be headed for another moontower. Nick pulled out the brochure he'd pocketed from Princeps' desk, showing all the tower locations, with two in particular circled. Was that where Josephine was?

Both of the circled towers were out toward the south edge of town, in less populated areas. One was at Zilker Park, the site of the natural swimming springs. The other was labeled as the State Deaf & Dumb Institute. The electric streetcar line would take him almost directly there. The car lumbered forward, not at all quickly enough for Nick's liking. It stopped at every intersection even though no one was getting off or on.

At the seventh stop, they were within sight of the car in front of them on the same line. Nick jumped off the slowing trolley, sprinted to the one ahead of them, and jumped aboard, paying the startled conductor another nickel. If he could do that a few more times, this would be the fastest, most expensive trolley ride in Austin history; hopefully faster than a horse.

Nick tried to come up with a plan for when he got where he was going. The tower at the Deaf and Dumb Institute was close to the streetcar line, just two blocks off of it. Zilker Park was another two miles west from there. If he chose the wrong one, he might never see Josephine again. Zilker Park was probably a more secluded location for whatever kind of ritual Princeps had planned. But it made the most sense to start searching at the institute because he could be there more quickly.

But how would he find Josephine, even if he chose the right tower? Nick thought about the newspaper clipping. If Princeps believed the lights attracted some kind of being, then he would probably have her near the tower itself. On the tower? Nick remembered from newspaper reports that there was a pulley system going up the center of the structures, like a dumbwaiter, for maintenance men to access the lighting elements. Maybe he-

Nick heard gasps from the other passengers. They were looking back and pointing, and he turned to see what had caused the uproar. A blinding light shone out from behind them, well above the tops of the tallest buildings, piercing the night sky. The Hyde Park moontower had been lit, and the others were beginning to come on too. Time was running out. Nick muttered a prayer that he was heading the right way.

The streetcar crossed the muddy and torpid Colorado River. At least now, across the official barrier to the gritty south side of town, there were fewer stops.

As the car slowed at Gibson Street, Nick jumped off and ran. A block ahead of him, the institute's land began. The brochure showed the moontower to be somewhere on the southeast corner of the campus. But now that he was close, it was easy to follow the array of inch-thick steel cables that ran from street level up to the still unlit tower, holding it in place like Gulliver tied by the Lilliputians.

There was no fence around the institute's land, on this end anyway. The area was lightly wooded with young pine trees like a neglected yard, and Nick found what seemed to be a footpath leading from the sidewalk into the interior, in the general direction of the tower. As he entered the wooded section, the crickets and frogs ceased their incessant croaking and warbling in his vicinity. The sound was really only noticeable in its absence.

As he drew into the trees, any starlight was blocked and Nick wished he had a lantern. The path twisted and branches raked at him. After he tore down a few spider webs with his face, he began walking with his hands stretched in front of him. He was no longer sure the path was headed in the correct direction, and he couldn't see the support cables above to follow them. He made and broke several deals with himself that he would turn back if he didn't see something in twenty more steps.

Finally, the narrow trail opened into a clearing of mowed grass at least fifty feet across. The smell of cut pine trees was strong; the insects buzzed as if Nick were of no concern. The opening wasn't much brighter than the trail he'd come from, but he was fairly certain that the gray mass in the center of the circle was the base of the moontower.

The gray structure stretched into the darkness above him. As he gazed up at it, the arc lights suddenly pulsed on. It was immediately blinding, the six white hot spots blotting out the entire night sky. With the light came a droning electrical buzz that was nearly as loud as the forest sounds around him. Nick looked away and his vision began to return. The clearing was lit, but without the colors of daytime, everything in shades of white and black. Bits of ash fell from the lights and drifted to the ground like gray snow.

Gradually the mass of shadows at the base of the tower resolved into something the size of a human figure. He sprinted forward and found her. It was Josephine! Nick let out a cry of relief. She was lying inert, her mouth gagged and her hands bound behind her, tied to the framework of the tower. She looked bad; the nightgown she wore was torn and stained red. Blood, dried dark, matted her hair and traced lines from her temple down her cheek. But it was her! He'd found her, and he was never going to leave her again. He placed his ear close to her face and tried to pause his own breathing while he listened. Finally he felt more than heard the slow, faint breaths coming from her.

"Oh, thank God," he sighed. "Josephine," he called, as he pulled the cloth gag off her mouth. But she didn't respond. She seemed to be asleep or unconscious. He spoke to her anyway: "Josie, I'm here. I'm going to get you out of here. We're going to go far away, where this will never happen again." He pulled out his pocketknife and began sawing at the ropes that held her hands, being careful not to cut her in the deep shadows under the tower. After too long a moment of working on them, he felt the ropes where he'd been cutting. Nick's pocket knife wasn't making any progress on her bonds. He sawed away some more and still felt no mark on the ropes. He checked the edge of his knife; it was as sharp as ever, but totally ineffective. Was she tied with steel cable? He dropped the useless knife and felt around the bonds until he came to a knot. It felt like normal rope, and he struggled to untie it.

The crickets and frogs stopped their twangy humming all at once. Behind him, a horse snorted. Nick turned and saw a black horse stride silently into the clearing. When it stopped, a figure dressed in black slowly dismounted.

"Leave her alone," a familiar low scratchy voice commanded. "You are not permitted to be here. Step away from her now, while you can."

Nick stayed crouched next to Josephine and pulled the revolver out of his right jacket pocket. Pointing it at Princeps' chest, he yelled back, "You stay where you are, or I'll shoot you where you stand!"

The man chuckled. "Why, Mr. Raeburn, I'm truly impressed that you got here so quickly. I expected to have this tower to myself for the evening." As he spoke, he took a few limping steps forward, using his cane heavily.

Nick cocked the hammer back on the revolver. "I won't warn you again. Don't come any closer or I'll shoot you."

Princeps glanced at the gun, then at the knife on the ground. "Oh, you won't cut through the rope with that knife. It's not made of normal hemp." He looked up at the moontower, and then took another step forward. "I don't really have time for any more of your interruptions."

Nick held the gun steady at Princeps' chest and squeezed the trigger. Despite himself, he closed his eyes against the impending flash and explosion. Instead there was only a click. He opened his eyes and looked at the gun. The hammer was down. He pulled the trigger again. Another click, and no explosion.

Princeps closed the distance between them unbelievably quickly for an old man, and then effortlessly kicked the knife away toward the tower. Nick drew his arm back to use the pistol as a club, but before he could strike, Princeps reached out and placed his hand on Nick's chest and spat a word that sounded like "fillet." Nick was thrust backward like the time he was kicked by a horse. He tried to use his arms to break his fall, but was unable to move them; his entire body was slack. He hit the ground hard, landing on his right shoulder, the breath knocked out of him.

Princeps stepped back shakily, using the cane to steady himself. Whatever he'd done to Nick seemed to cost him. He kept speaking, but quieter, seemingly to himself. "You think I've lived this long by being careless? By letting guns work in my vicinity? Certainly, you'd suspect I'd take care of that, what with a hundred policemen looking for me. That piece of metal will be quite useless until I leave. By which time you may want to use it on yourself, after you see what's about to happen." He shook out both hands as if flinging something off them, then added: "I do feel sorry for you. Well, both of you, really. But it can't be helped. I didn't ask for you to intrude on my business. I'm not even sure how you were able to enter this clearing. My wardings should have kept you out."

Nick got his breath back. He still couldn't move his arms or legs, but he could definitely still feel pain in them. The insistent throbbing in his shoulder was sharp enough to be a broken collarbone.

"Mr. Raeburn, I must thank you for your family's donation to procure the moontowers. I lobbied the mayor for years, but it was never going to happen without private donations. And I couldn't afford to pay for them all myself. At any rate, it looked better with a well-known family like yours contributing to the cause. So, it's only fitting that you'll be here to witness their true implementation." Princeps grabbed Nick under the armpits and tried to drag him closer to the base of the tower, but Nick's body barely moved, despite Princeps' straining exertion. Cursing in annoyance, Princeps grabbed Nick's left arm and lashed the wrist to the tower's frame.

Princeps hobbled back to his horse. He caught his breath for a moment before pulling a brown leather pouch out of the saddlebags. He returned and knelt in front of the stump of a tree that must've been felled to make room of the moontower. On top of the stump, he placed two candles and a metal bowl.

He lit the candles with a match, and then rose and approached Josephine. As he walked, he pulled out a small scalpel that he wore on a thong around his neck. Nick tested his limbs and found they would move, but they felt weak and uncoordinated, like their circulation had been cut off. Princeps reached out with his left hand and tilted Josephine's head back, exposing her smooth neck.

He's going to cut her, Nick thought. Not knowing what

else to do, Nick called out, "Why are you doing this?"

Princeps stopped and a smile crept over his face. "You might as well know what you're about to witness. You may be the first spectator in a thousand years to see it. Normally, only the sacrificer and the victim are present," he said, looking at Josephine.

He turned back to Nick, speaking louder now. "There are ancient beings that were here long before us. They are mostly unconcerned with us. We are like insects to them, and they seem to be bored with our kind. But the unnatural light of the moontowers draws their curiosity. Once they are looking this way, my ceremony will call their attention down on me. I will use that opportunity to ask them for more time."

Nick tried moving his fingers again, with no more success. He needed to keep Princeps talking. "More... time?"

Princeps laughed derisively. "I can't even explain it to one such as you." He looked toward the sky and took a deep breath, and evidently decided to try. "If an infant was born but was never fed, it would die in a few days, never knowing what it was like to eat. You and your kind are the same. You are born and live your fourscore years, and never know what it is that would sustain you for longer. This is what the Oldest Ones grant to me." His eyes closed almost fully at the thought. "It is a sustenance that is fulfilling beyond description." He looked up toward the lights, oblivious to the cinders falling on his face. "It staves off age like food banishes starvation." Then he turned back to the girl, readying his knife.

Nick realized he had found something Princeps seemed to really want to talk about, and he tried to keep him engaged. "But why would they give you this, this sustenance?" Nick asked, finding that he could flex his fingers individually again, if still weakly.

Princeps grunted a laugh. "Why favor me, you mean?

Someone so vile in your eyes? The Oldest Ones are not constrained by your morality, boy," he said, standing up straighter to look down upon Nick. "But they understand fealty. And commitment. And the ultimate commitment a human can show, from the earliest days, is to sacrifice his own kin." Princeps knelt before Josephine, placing his black cane on the ground. "So I collect blood from girls when they are small. Sometimes I get it when they are born. This girl's I got when she was in a farm accident as a child." He tilted her head back and ran a finger across her exposed neck. "Once I collect it, I mix my own blood with theirs. It is what ties them to me. This blood mixture sits for years. And so when I come back to them years later, the Oldest Ones perceive the girls to be my offspring... that I am sacrificing my own child to them. And just as important, I have learned how to ask them my favor properly. I've learned the songs and the ceremonies that they respond to." He drew the knife back.

The image of collected blood reminded Nick of the talisman he'd taken, the Egyptian cross still in his jacket. "Stop!" he commanded. Princeps jerked his head in alarm and gave Nick an annoyed look. Nick fumbled awkwardly with his right hand into his left jacket pocket. Princeps did not seem concerned but continued to watch him. Nick's hand dug through boiled shrimp, and finally came out with the cross. "Leave her alone and back away, or I'll... I'll destroy this."

Princeps' eyes went wide. "Mr. Raeburn, you are full of surprises," he snorted, picking up his cane and standing to face Nick. "The girl was resisting so much while I was packing up my accouterments this morning that I forgot that particular piece." He nodded at the cross. "I'll admit I was fairly distressed at not having it, but I didn't have time to go back for it." He hobbled to Nick's side, stopping just out of arm's reach, staring eagerly at the cross. "The ceremony would work without it, but I am pleased to see you've brought it for me."

"Walk away or I'll break it," Nick said, not at all sure he had the strength to break anything.

"Well, you do as you must, but I haven't got all night. The Oldest Ones are not patient." Princeps turned dismissively back to Josephine, but then whirled back, striking Nick's arm with his wooden cane.

The blow fell on Nick's forearm and the pain was white hot agony, but Nick held on to the cross. He clenched his fist with all his might until he felt the cross crack. "I warned you!" he croaked. One of the arms of the cross had broken off, and a thick black liquid, like tar, was oozing out of the hole.

Princeps looked furious and began hitting him around the shoulders and head with the cane, all the while reaching for the cross. The impacts rained around Nick's face, and with his left hand still tied to the tower, he was helpless to defend himself. Finally, after a sharp blow to his temple, Nick drew his arm back and threw the talisman toward the edge of the clearing.

"You idiot! Not on the ground!" yelled Princeps, limping hurriedly toward the spot where the talisman had flown.

Nick lay back, exhausted. His head, neck and shoulders throbbed. His left eye was closed and wouldn't open. Blood seeped into his right eye, but he didn't care enough to wipe it away. Through the blood obscuring his vision, he saw Princeps recover the cross from where it hung on a lower branch of a thorny bush, looking over his shoulder as if he expected pursuit. The old man returned and placed the broken talisman around Josephine's neck. Nick yanked ineffectually at the rope holding his left hand while Princeps retrieved the metal bowl from the makeshift altar. The old man began humming a low tune, and slowly, delicately, he slid the scalpel into the side of Josephine's neck.

Nick cried out, but Princeps didn't even flinch this time. A fine trickle of blood ran down from the cut, then dripped from Josephine's collarbone into the waiting bowl.

"She can't hear you," Princeps said matter-of-factly over his shoulder. "The herbs she's inhaled to prepare her for the Oldest Ones have cut her off from this world." He sliced his own finger and held the dripping wound over the bowl. Returning to the tree stump, he reached into the leather pouch and retrieved dried leaves, which he crumbled onto the candle to his right, causing bright blue sparks to rise up from the flames. He started singing a low warbling song as he held the bowl over the candle on his left.

Nick tried to make out words in the plaintive song, but they were indistinct, and concentrating on it began to lull him into a sort of trance. The clearing took on a hazy look, like something seen on the other side of a campfire. He felt a pressure coming down from above him. The light of the moontower flickered as if it was being blown out.

Nick's ears popped as the pressure increased, as if he were swimming too deep under water, and he felt an intense desire to flee. His right arm reached up unbidden to struggle with the rope holding his left arm to the tower. For an instant he had a vision of a fox trap he'd seen as a boy, with only a fox's leg left in it. The sensation of pressure was so unsettling he was actually considering whether he could chew through his wrist. Princeps' song grew louder, and so deep it made Nick's chest vibrate. It seemed to be coming from all around.

Princeps put down the bowl and raised both hands over his head, fists clenched. The pressure in Nick's ears reduced, but he could feel that it increased over Princeps, making him appear blurry and indistinct. Princeps' mouth moved, as if he was saying something, no longer singing the song, yet the song went on like a sustained echo.

Suddenly Princeps stood, and in his hand was a small

black stick with a sharp tip. As he limped toward the tower, Nick felt the pressure come closer again, and heard Josephine gasp. She slowly moved her head like she was being pestered by a wasp. Nick could tell by her hazy appearance that the pressure was now centered on her. Then it came back to him, and his ears buzzed. He was aware of a presence within his own mind, questioning and probing. There was nothing he could do, it seemed to press his own thoughts flat against the sides of his mind as it explored.

Nick closed his eyes in an effort to hold on to what was him. But instead of seeing familiar darkness, he was aware of being in a limitless dim gray expanse that curved away to whiteness in every direction. He perceived a faint afterimage of the things around him: the ground, the forest, the moontower, but they were insubstantial, dark gray against lighter gray, and strangely flat. The light at the top of the tower was a cold bright spot that didn't illuminate its surroundings. The song was in this place too, seeming to be sung by thousands of low voices, everywhere, not coming from any particular direction.

He felt an enormous consciousness looking down on him, whatever down meant here. When he tried to turn his attention to it, it was not something he could see so much as a warping of the area near it, like seeing the wake behind a boat, without seeing the boat. He tried to look more closely at this overwhelming presence but he couldn't make himself, as if he was involuntarily flinching away from a too-bright light or a too-loud sound. But he knew when the Oldest One noticed him. It concentrated its attention on his own psyche, and he felt small and insignificant. Lacking.

Nick became aware of two other, small presences near him in this place. They were on the same scale as himself. One seemed familiar, and feminine. He understood that it was Josephine, her mind. He could feel her presence, but he knew he was seeing her through the perceptions of the overwhelming Oldest One, and she seemed to be a swirling blue orb, the way a full moon looks through clouds. He perceived her fear and confusion emanating from her. Then the inescapable attention turned to the other presence. This one was older, shriveled and hard, a misshapen scarlet stone. Princeps. Hate radiated from this one. Hate and an overriding fear of death. Then Nick saw himself through the perception of the Oldest One. He was manifested as a small pale orange sphere of light, also radiating fear, but this was not a fear for his own life.

The alien attention turned back to the hard red presence. This one wanted something, demanded it. Wanted more life, and was willing to trade the life of its own offspring to get it. But both of the young orbs seemed to be its offspring. The red presence was confused and angered: it didn't think the orange mote should be here at all. Princeps' anger was like that of a child who thinks he might not get what he wants.

The unbearable pressure returned to Nick and his own thoughts mingled with those of the Oldest One. At its bidding, Nick began to experience his own memories. Nick tried to close them, hold them to himself, but he didn't even know how to operate those muscles. He saw Princeps at the moontower debut, then Josephine, out in the bright sun, hanging laundry. Then dizzying confusion as he experienced visions that weren't his own. Josephine's memories of a young Nick. Nick falling into the thresher, and the blood, so much blood. Josephine reaching in to pull him out and being cut terribly herself, their blood mingling as she pulled him to safety. The doctor's assistant mopping up the blood, then limping away to wring out the red towels into a pail. Limping away, and looking back at her. Nick inhaled sharply through clenched teeth when he realized what he was seeing: Princeps, collecting her blood, inadvertently collecting both of their blood. The Oldest One registered the shock and anger from the mote that was Princeps, beseeching the Other to grant it more life, insisting on it.

With a wrenching effort, Nick tore his eyes open, bringing himself back to the clearing, and saw Princeps reaching for Josephine with the black spike. Nick flung his arm out to stop him, but was several feet short of being able to reach her. He stretched out, heedless of the cords biting into his wrist, pulling, willing his skin to tear so his arm would come free. The pain began to white his vision out, and he closed his eyes.

He was back in the gray expanse, again participating in the terrible awareness of the ancient Other. Nick understood that the Oldest One could not always peer inside the little ones like himself, only under certain conditions. It perceived their different emotions like scents or tastes. And it had found a new flavor. Not the fear of a thing selfishly dreading its own death, that was familiar, and stale. This new one was fear for another's pain, and it was honeyed and savory. It pleased the Other, brought it joy. Much more palatable than the old greedy longing. Now with something to compare it to, it found the old fear loathsome, and wanted less of it. It reached out to push the one that stunk of putrid fear away. Just a little push. Shove it aside. The gentlest nudge, and the red mote shrieked in agony, and then went out, gone from the dim expanse. And with it, the connection to the smaller, prettier ones was severed.

Nick's eyes flew open in shock. He looked around in the dimness and realized he was screaming. He stopped. His vision was normal; the low song was gone. Josephine was next to him, sitting up now. Princeps lay in front of him in a crumpled heap, not moving, looking very frail and impossibly shriveled. A slow rising and falling of his chest was the only sign he was still alive.

Nick looked to his left hand, still tied to the tower. The rope now felt thin and rotted, and he broke free without much effort. He went to Josephine, who looked up at him through heavy-lidded eyes, breathing rapidly. He found he was able to break her bonds easily too. "Josie! Josie, are you hurt?" She slowly shook her head no.

"What just happened?" Nick asked, disoriented.

Her words came as if from far away, like she was describing something she had dreamed: "It was like when he came for me before, like that, with the giant mind pressing down. Did you feel that as well?" She looked at him, her eyes searching, on the verge of tears. Nick nodded, and she went on. "And Count Lune started speaking to it, asking it for more life. But I don't think you were supposed to be in there. You surprised him by being there."

Nick brushed the hair back out of Josephine's face. "When Princeps ... Count Lune took your blood, from the accident at the ranch, he took my blood too. Maybe he didn't realize that," said Nick. "Or maybe he thought it wouldn't matter, since I wouldn't be at the ceremony..."

Josephine stood shakily, and held tightly onto Nick. "And it felt like once the giant thing got to see Count Lune in comparison to regular people, non-horrible people, it realized it had been helping the wrong side."

Nick stood up and walked toward the old man, who was not stirring.

"What are you doing?" Josephine called out.

"Ending this," Nick said, recovering his pocket knife from the dirt.

Nick knelt by the wreck of a man. He pressed the knife blade to Princeps' soft throat.

He thought about what it must take to transform your consciousness from a glowing, swirling orb into a shriveled cinder. The Oldest One hadn't killed Princeps when it had the chance; it took pity on him. No reason to kill something just because you could. Nick pulled the knife away and stood. Where the blade had been, a bright red drop of blood swelled from a tiny cut, and then ran down the loose skin of the old man's neck to drop onto the pale dry dirt.

Nick watched the blood soak into the thirsty soil, and noticed the insects stop their buzzing abruptly, but the silence was broken when the black horse began rearing and stamping, straining against the bridle that tied it to a tree branch.

Nick turned to Josephine and helped her to her feet, examining her for injuries, but stopped as small dark shapes appeared, moving near Princeps. It wasn't clear if they were coming from the forest or up out of the ground itself. They were armored and many-legged, like small black horseshoe crabs. Their glistening shells were adorned with what might be runes, and they made a clicking noise like bony pincers closing. They swarmed over Princeps and completely covered him, until he was a writhing mound. There came a groan, but it was quickly swallowed up as the clicking grew louder and faster. Nick and Josephine staggered several steps back. But almost as soon as it began, the mound shrank and the creatures became less distinct, until they seemed to be just shadows, and then nothing at all. All they left behind was a small black pile that looked like ashes.

Josephine turned to Nick, her eyes round with terror. Nick looked for any signs of the crawling things near them. "Mama Queenie said there were spirit creatures chasing him to collect what he owes them, but his power was able to hold them back. I guess his debt has been paid."

"You talked to Mama Queenie?" she said, a smile slowly brightening her face like clouds lifting. "I wish I could have seen that."

"I'll tell you all about it. But not here. Let's get away from here," Nick said, putting his arm around her.

They walked into the forest together, leaving the buzzing moontower behind.

* * *

They didn't speak as they walked back through the dark woods. Once they were in the open air of the street, Nick gave Josie his jacket to wear over her nightgown, but he couldn't do anything about her bare feet. He wondered what he must look like himself.

He was exhausted and hungry, but he was walking hand in hand with Josephine through the quiet streets. Nick found he didn't have anything to say that was more important than the silence.

It wasn't until they approached Congress Avenue that they heard voices talking and laughing, growing louder as if a party was quickly getting closer. The streetcar stopped in front of them with a squealing sound of overburdened brakes, and the obviously drunk crowd yelled for them to get aboard.

Nick's hands shook as he dug out ten cents for two fares.

Helpful arms pulled them up into the packed car. Once on board, Nick and Josephine stood side by side, drinking from offered bottles and watching the city rush toward them with the wind, the moontowers still lighting the sky like stationary fireworks.

Then, one by one, the towers began to go out. The passengers raised their flasks and glasses and shouted and sang as each one faded, until only one light was left. Nick put his arm around Josephine's waist. He tried to think of something clever to say, how it was her turn to save his life next. But instead he kissed her, and she kissed him back. And the crowd cheered again.

* * * * *

Tim Powers is one of my favorite authors. One of the things he does that I enjoy the most is to take actual historical events and come up with supernatural explanations for them. Ever since I read The Anubis Gates *and* The Stress of Her Regard, *I've wanted to try my hand at a story like that.*

In 2015 the 99% Invisible *podcast introduced me to the Servant Girl Annihilator, one of the first serial killers, and to the idea that many people think Austin installed its moontowers in response to him, even though they arrived ten years after the murders stopped. I started wondering: what if the moontowers were related to the Servant Girl Annihilator, but in exactly the opposite way everyone assumed?*

Thanks for reading. If you enjoyed this book, please leave me an honest review here:

www.amazon.com

Sign up for my free email list and be the first to hear about what's coming next, along with sneak peeks and free short stories.

Sign up now:

www.benconceivable.com/newsletter

Acknowledgments:

This collection would never have gotten off of the ground at all without the encouragement of my wife and family. And it would be far less comprehensible without multiple early readings by Kim and my Storytime compadres David and Matt. And it would be far less readable without the editing efforts of Lee at Ocean's Edge Editing and Joseph at the Syntax Soviet. Finally, the striking cover is from Domi at Inspired Cover Designs.

Thanks so much for everyone who helped!